The Fairy Lights

First published in 2022 by Leilanie Stewart

The Fairy Lights Copyright © 2022 Leilanie Stewart

ISBN: 9781739952358

Front cover design 'ghost on stairwell' © 2022 Leilanie Stewart
Rear cover photograph 'Friar's Bush Graveyard' © 2022 Leilanie Stewart
Internal free image download from www.clipartkey.com

Thank you for supporting independent publishing.

Website: www.leilaniestewart.com
F: facebook.com/leilaniestewartauthor
Twitter: @leilaniestewart
Instagram: @leilaniestewartauthor

The Fairy Lights

Leilanie Stewart

Also by Leilanie Stewart

Belfast Ghosts Series

Book 1: The Blue Man

Book 2: The Fairy Lights

Other novels

The Buddha's Bone

Gods of Avalon Road

To my two fellow horror lovers, Joe and KJ, who help keep the fire of my imagination burning brightly.

Chapter one

Aisling taped the last fairy light to the narrow stairwell of the redbrick Edwardian terraced house that she had called home for the past three months. The multi-coloured lights snaked up the handrail, around the bannister on the landing above, across the ceiling and down the other side of the stairs towards the hallway. They had a battery compartment, USB port and plug in attachment, but for now electricity would do. She plugged them in and slid the switch to the right, making the lights blink.

No: too garish; and it was bound to give her a headache. What if one of her guests had epilepsy and the blinking fairy lights triggered a fit? It was a serious consideration; after all, a seizure had eventually led to her own mum's passing. Too much risk. She slid the switch through the middle setting – off – and over to the left side, which put the fairy lights at a static 'on' setting. Perfect. She stood back and admired her handiwork with a smile. A bit of festive colour would add seasonal cheer to her party, the first she had ever hosted.

Before she left the house to get party supplies, Aisling switched off all the Christmas lights: tree in the living room, front window LED Santa, snowman and snowflake, nutcracker lights strung across the kitchen and lastly, the fairy lights running up the stairwell. She pulled on her boots and coat and set off up the street to the main road to do some shopping.

When Aisling returned half an hour later, she was laden with two canvas bags full of drinks – both alcoholic and non-alcoholic – as well as party treats. She had tried to buy as wide a range of food as the local convenience store would allow for: vegan canapēs; a selection of Christmas cheese nibbles; a gluten-free yuletide log and of course, the all-time party favourite food, cocktail sausages. She fumbled with the latch key to the door and squeezed into the narrow hallway sideways to allow room for the two bulky bags without squashing anything.

Aisling stopped without shutting the front door and stared up the stairwell. The fairy lights were switched on. Hadn't she turned everything off before she had left the house? Yes, she was pretty sure she had. She went over it all in her head: tree; LED lights; string kitchen lights; fairy lights. Yes, she was positive she had switched everything off.

There was only one explanation for it; the fairy lights had to be faulty. The three settings of the switch were indeed close to each other on the plug: left for on, middle for off and right for blinking. Maybe a minor malfunction of the wires allowed it to switch on by itself. Not to worry; Aisling set down her shopping carrier bags in the hallway, pushed the front door shut with her foot and traipsed up the stairs to have a look.

Aisling stared at the switch on the plug. It had been flicked to the left.

But that was impossible. She was positive that she had slid the switch to the middle setting – off – when she had left the house not half an hour before.

There couldn't possibly be an intruder in the house, could there? A chill came over her as she set about checking every room. All the windows were shut and nothing looked disturbed. Besides, even if a burglar had broken into the house – in half an hour, no less – why would they have turned on the fairy lights as a marker that they had been and gone? It made no sense.

Aisling stopped on the landing and looked up. A small hatch opened into the attic. It measured maybe twelve by eighteen inches; narrow, but enough for a person to fit through. What if a person was living up there and sneaking about the house when she was out? It was an Edwardian, two-up, two-down 'parlour' house in Stranmillis Village in Belfast, probably built over a hundred years ago, judging by fact that it had a built in coal-bunker out in the back yard that now housed the boiler. It had a shed too, a built-in brickwork compartment next to the coal-bunker that was covered with a corrugated iron roof. The shed had once been, most likely, an outside toilet when neither electricity nor internal plumbing were commonplace. Such an old house probably gave access to roof spaces and other nooks and crannies where a person could hide.

The thought was unsettling, but that wasn't why Aisling ruled it out. No, she ruled it out for another reason; if a person, or persons, were living in her attic space then food or possessions would have gone missing. Nothing had been stolen, moved or misplaced in the three months since she had moved in. Furthermore, she was a Queen's University student like most of the people living on her street. Like many other students she could think of, Aisling was broke. What good would it do for a person to live in the roof-space above an undergraduate History with Irish student with more debt than money to their name?

No; *Occam's Razor. The simplest explanation is usually the best one.* What did Aisling's gut feeling tell her about the mystery of the fairy lights switching on by themselves?

That the fairy lights hadn't malfunctioned. They hadn't switched on by themselves.

That no living person was living in her attic.

No *living person.*

Aware of the chill still lingering around her shoulders, Aisling hunched them close to herself and rubbed her arms for warmth as she glanced over the bannister at the fairy lights, shining benignly at her. If only they could speak to her, to tell her in their own words what had happened. Who – or what – had switched them on?

Chapter two

Aisling walked home from her only lecture that day. Student life could be so easy sometimes. Easy and difficult. She couldn't deny she was lonely. Some of her classmates had seemed keen the previous week when she had told them about her party coming up on Saturday. In the three months since term had started, she hadn't managed to find anyone she particularly bonded with. Sure, they were nice. There was Liv who was loud and bubbly, and had a big, bouncy mane of blonde curls to match; but seemed a bit too brash for Aisling's taste, aside from amusing her in the lecture theatre with funny quips about whatever professor was speaking. There was Eoin, all black hair and black-framed glasses who was moody and sensitive, more on her wavelength in some ways; but he just wasn't – just wasn't... Wasn't what? Fun enough? Or was it that he seemed like a mopey sort of friend, a bit too needy for her comfort. Aisling didn't mind lovers who were needier, more clingy people, but it didn't make for good friend-material. Not that she had a lover in her life either. Friends or lovers, anything would do at the moment. Beggars couldn't be choosers. Aisling sighed as she turned into her small, overgrown front garden with its tall holly hedges, welcoming her home alone, as usual.

As soon as she opened her front door, a chill seized her body. The fairy lights shone across the stairwell, creating pools of blue, green, pink and yellow over the cream-coloured wallpaper. Fear pierced Aisling's mind as she marched across the hallway; dread filled her legs, heavy with the anticipation of what she would find and she thudded up the stairs. Her hand reached towards the plug of the fairy lights, fingers splayed, ready to face the truth–

The switch had been flicked to the left. Someone – or something – had pushed that small, black piece of plastic over to the left side, thereby turning an inoffensive object into the biggest threat Aisling had felt in her whole life. For now, there was no more doubt in her mind. Her house was haunted.

***

Aisling rested her chin on her knuckles. Her fingers were latticed over her cup of tea, her elbows perched on the kitchen counter. She enjoyed the steam rising up and warming her palms, massaging her face. It provided temporary respite from the dreaded realisation that upstairs, a ghost resided in her house. Tea seemed to soothe everything. She didn't know how, or why. Maybe it reminded her of early mornings with her mum, having heart-to-hearts over a cuppa while her brother and dad were still in bed. If only her mum were there with her now to give her comfort, tell her she was being silly. Ghosts didn't exist, did they? If they did, then mum was one too. Did such a notion comfort her, or add more to her repertoire of terrifying possibilities that had opened out over the past forty-eight hours? Yep; frightened her. The spiritual world – if it existed – was alien and terrifying.

Wasn't the thought of a person living in her attic and sneaking around more likely than a ghost switching on the fairy lights? Yes – in theory. It defied logic, but Aisling's gut feeling, her deepest, most buried instinct within the realms of her subconscious, was telling her that a paranormal explanation provided the true answer for what was happening in her house.

Aisling gulped her tea down, burning her throat. Her eyes watered. Pain radiated across her tongue. Physical discomfort was good; it reminded her that she was in the here and now. She was alive and in control. This was her house. She would get to the bottom of it, solve the mystery of the fairy lights.

She steeled her nerves to walk up the stairs. One step: coolness enveloped her. Second step: getting frigid. Third step: the noticeable drop in temperature caused a cloud of condensation to fill the air with her exhalation. Coldness seemed to pool in certain areas, welling on the stairs and landing.

Nobody else was in the house apart from her, but it wasn't what every sensation in her body told her. The fine hairs on her arm stood on end. Goosebumps prickled across her skin. Her muscles tensed and adrenaline coursed, ready for fight or flight. Flight, if a ghost were actually to materialise on the stairwell above, or the landing. She had dismissed the coldness as being due to draughts from the attic, poor insulation letting all the heat out; any excuse that suited, really. Now she had run out of excuses. A ghost shared her home and brought with it an ethereal coldness.

"Hello? Who's there? Show yourself."

Aisling's frightened voice echoed in her own ears, an octave higher than how she would normally speak. She cleared her throat; this was her house. No spectre would force her out of a place that not only belonged to her family, but that she had made her home for the next three years.

"Do you want to get my attention for some reason – is that why you've been switching on my fairy lights? So that I know you're there?"

No answer. Of course there wouldn't be. A wave of embarrassment washed over Aisling; how ludicrous to be speaking in an otherwise empty house and expecting a reply.

She whipped her phone out of her pocket. There was a pause before her dad answered. "Hello, dad? It's me. Listen, I have a question about the house. This is going to sound really strange."

"What is it, love? Did something happen? You weren't broken into?"

"No, don't worry, it's nothing like that." Aisling sighed. "Did you ever live in this house at any point?"

"Well, sure. I haven't always been renting it out. I lived in it when I was studying Economics at Queen's in the nineties." Her dad guffawed. "It's sort of becoming a family tradition to spend your student days there. Maybe you can get your own kids to spend their undergrad days in it when they go to Queen's, or Ulster University, someday."

Better to ignore the awkward conversation about kids. "Dad, do you believe in ghosts?"

A pause. "You know I do, love. I like to think your mum is still with us every day. I talk to her in the mornings when I'm getting ready for work, and last thing at night."

She rolled her eyes, thankful that he couldn't see her. "That's different – I miss mum too. But I meant, like, do you believe that ghosts can be a physical presence? You know, that they can make places seem colder just by being there and that they can tamper with objects in someone's house?"

"What's this about, sweetheart? Are you worried that the old house, is haunted?"

When dad put it that way, it sounded absolutely ridiculous. "In a word, yes."

"Well, now that you mention it, we did used to joke about old Jimbo when we were living there, me and a mate of mine. I stayed in the master bedroom at the front of the house and my mate Stevie stayed in the back bedroom, the one you picked."

As her dad's words sunk in, Aisling gulped. "Who was Jimbo?"

"Ach, probably nothing, love. I don't want you worrying your wee head about it." Dad's voice took on an exaggerated whine, which it did when he was pleading with her to believe him about a topic. She knew him too well though, and it had the opposite effect.

"No, tell me," she said. "Jimbo – so I'm guessing some fella named Jim used to live in the house?"

"It's just hearsay, you know how it goes. Every other auld house or building in Belfast has a story about being haunted – you can't throw a rock without some place or other having a ghost." Dad forced a laugh, but Aisling heard the nervousness in his voice.

"Listen, dad. If you don't tell me about Jim, then I'll find out myself."

Dad hesitated then sighed. "You always were so headstrong, just like your mum. Alright then. When your Granda bought the house back in 82, he said the auld man who sold it to him gave it to him so cheap because of Jimbo. These houses round here would have sold for maybe £28,000 back in the late seventies, early eighties, but he got it for only £10,000. Apparently a man called Jim Murphy had died in the house, around the turn of the century, 1900s, you know."

"Jim Murphy? How did he die?"

"The man who sold it to your Granda never mentioned that. He mumbled some keek or other about how the spirit was a bit restless and liked to make its presence known from time to time. Just to assert dominance, I'm sure. It's a shame about the rumours, you know. These houses today would fetch upwards of £150,000, but if I wanted to sell ours, I'd be lucky to get £120,000 I think, all because of Jimbo."

"Alrighty dad, ta for the info. I'll see you soon. Not long til I'm off for Christmas."

A pause. "Are you sure you're okay, sweetheart?"

"Aye, don't worry about me. A bit spooked, but I'll live. Love you."

"Love you too."

She ended the call and tucked the phone back in her pocket. A cold chill tickled her shoulders and neck, static electricity raising every hair until it stood on end. Jimbo, the owner of her house back in Edwardian times was stuck in limbo on earth. She needed to get in contact with him. Not only that; she needed to get him out of her house.

Chapter three

A isling sat cross-legged at the top of the stairs. The hallway mirror, which she had taken off the nail, was now propped against the newel post to the left of the stairs. The fairy lights glowed with innocent brilliance and she took comfort in their brightness; more so, because if her plan worked, she would soon be very scared indeed. Terrified, in fact. If her plan worked, Jimbo would look out of the mirror at her and she would see the face of the man who had been haunting her house since long before even her grandfather was born.

She placed her hands on the glass and saw a halo of condensation form around each finger. The top of the stairs where she sat was the coldest spot in the house; Aisling shuddered at the thought. She needed to be brave; this could take a long time, maybe even all night. She was prepared to do whatever it took.

Aisling looked in the mirror. Grey semi-circles arced under each of her brown eyes. Her dark brown hair was unkempt, messy around her shoulders and with a few strands sticking up on top of her head. Had she really been that worried about the unknown entity in her house? She smoothed her hair flat against her head, took a deep breath and started.

"Hello, Jim Murphy? If you are there, show me a sign."

Aisling stared hard at herself in the mirror, but nothing happened.

She sighed. How stupid was this, really? She felt like a flippin' numpty, sitting there at the top of the stairs, talking to herself in the mirror, trying to contact a ghost.

Aisling rubbed the inside corner of each eye with her thumb and index finger, massaging the bridge of her nose while she was at it. She really should have brought up a cup of tea to keep her warm; she hadn't even thought to bring a glass of water, never mind a nice, hot brew. Oh well. Fingers crossed Jimbo would materialise sooner rather than later.

What would help to contact the dead? She had heard that meditation worked to clear the mind, and in that sense, to get in touch with unseen energies. Aisling straightened her back. She pulled her right foot up onto her inner left thigh and placed her left foot on her right knee, getting herself into a lotus position. Yoga class hadn't helped to make friends, but it kept her body limber and her head centred.

Aisling closed her eyes and breathed in for a count of three through her nose, then out for a count of five through her mouth. In and out, each breath relaxing her body and opening her unconscious mind.

Air in for three, then out for five.

Three in, five out.

In, out.

She felt her own warm breath blow over her arms and legs, the air expelled from her chest heating her feet and toes.

A deep breath in and then a cold gust of air over her back, sending a shiver down her spine.

Aisling opened her eyes and caught sight of her panicked face in the mirror. An unseen presence had exhaled a cold breath of air from beyond the grave that had breezed along her back raising goosebumps in its wake. Her own breath caught in her throat. Now was the time to make contact.

"Jim Murphy, is that you?" Aisling focused her thoughts, in spite of the blood pounding in her ears, making her lightheaded. "You're known as Jimbo, aren't you?"

The mirror rocked, first left, then right, in time with the fairy lights flashing off then on. Aisling yelped and lifted both hands away from the mirror. She willed herself to be brave and put both palms back on the mirror, spreading her fingers wide on the glassy surface.

"Are you angry at me for being in your house, Jimbo?"

The mirror didn't move.

"Do you know this is my house now? My granddad bought it, it's been in my family for decades."

The mirror rocked: left then right. The fairy lights blinked off and back on.

"I guess that means, yes, you understand."

Mirror left then right, fairy lights off then on.

Aisling wiped her brow, surprised that sweat dotted her hairline despite the chill. Guess adrenaline did its own thing in the face of the unseen.

What did she know about ghosts? Not much. Until now, she hadn't believed in anything supernatural. If she had known a week before that she would be sitting there in her house, three weeks before Christmas, communing with the dead she would think herself entirely bonkers. Off her rocker, gaga to be precise. Yet, there she was, having a fully-fledged conversation with Jim Murphy, a resident who had died in her house a hundred years before. Not to mention the fact that she was on a roll with her questioning; Aisling forced her mind to think of new things to ask.

"Are you stuck here on earth and trying to find a way back to the afterlife?"

No movement from the mirror, no blinking of the fairy lights.

"Hmm." Aisling searched her own reflection. "Did you die in this house?"

No movement, or lights blinking.

Interesting; that wasn't what her dad had said. "So, you didn't die here, but you're haunting this house because it was yours when you lived on earth?"

The mirror rocked and the lights flashed off then on. Bingo. Aisling was starting to understand. In the glow of the fairy lights, she caught sight of her reflection with yellow, pink, blue and green spotlights across her face. Her gaze drifted behind her; the base of the mirror had shifted forwards showing a view of the attic hatch in the ceiling above. It had been closed earlier, but now was half open. In the darkness beyond, the fairy lights highlighted a man's face peering out through the hatch. He was a dense mass of dark grey, like shadow formed into a human shape. Deep-set eyes watched her and a wide mouth grinned. Aisling shrieked and fell forwards, down the stairs.

Chapter four

The front of Aisling's head throbbed. She massaged her forehead with forefinger and thumb; maybe that fall yesterday had knocked her head worse than she had realised. There was no bump at least, thanks to the bag of frozen peas that she had applied, wrapped in a tea towel.

Still, it wasn't as if she had concussion; *adulting* wasn't going to make her prone to hypochondria now that she wasn't living at home with her Dad to take care of her. Aisling made a mental note to take some ibuprofen when she went back inside. A silly old headache wasn't enough to quit a task midway through, and the garden was in *serious* need of some festive cheer. She weaved snowflake string lights over the hedge running adjacent to her house and across the top of the holly bush running parallel to the street.

"Ow!" Aisling's finger jumped to her mouth and she sucked the bloody dot that had sprung up on the tip. The holly leaves were sharper than she thought. "Who in their right mind grows a feckin' holly bush in their garden anyway? Bloody liability."

Maybe it was time to quit after all. Still sucking her bleeding finger, Aisling turned to go back inside. Before the porch roof obscured her view, she noted that the clouds were looking black and ominous in any event. Was it going to be another storm? She had lost track of how many storms there had been that autumn; too many. Ireland wasn't immune to the climate change that was battering other parts of the world even worse, in comparison. Though lately, all the storms had wreaked havoc on her house. For one, the wind always blew the attic hatches wide open, leaving the house bloody *Baltic*. Then two, it made the already-dodgy electrics flicker even worse. And three, there was a sinister sag in the plaster above the shower that she was sure would fall the next time torrential rain pelted the roof. As tight as dad could be with money, he would really need to pull out his thumb and get the whole bathroom damp-proofed now that it was going to be her home for the next three years.

Or was it? There was still the issue – problem – of Jimbo. Did she really want to share her home with a spirit for the next three years? Last night she had managed to sleep only through exhaustion after falling down the stairs and injuring herself. That was one night. How many other nights, sleepless nights, would she suffer in the knowledge that she shared her home with a restless spirit. One of them would have to go – and it wouldn't be her.

Mind you, Jimbo didn't mean her any harm, did he? She had asked him if he was angry and the mirror hadn't rocked. Was he a benign spirit, maybe even a tad lonely like she was?

Yes, she decided; that would have to suffice as an explanation in the meantime. Between a malicious poltergeist out to drive her insane or a benign and somewhat lonely ghost, only lingering in the spirit – pun intended – of friendship, Aisling liked to think the latter was the case. If Jimbo were a friendly ghost, then she could live with that; at least until she found out more about him, or how to help him leave earth and go into the light.

Aisling walked with much lighter steps and a happier heart as she went back inside her house. What if Jimbo even became a housemate of sorts, a spectral sub-letter? Aisling chortled to herself at the thought as she made her way towards the living room.

A dull thud upstairs jolted her from her musings. Speak of the Devil; Jimbo must have wanted to tell her something. Aisling about-turned on her heel and went upstairs.

As expected, the attic hatch was open by a couple of inches. Her gaze dropped from the open hatch to the carpet on the landing where a small, pocket-sized book lay. She picked it up and blew a thick layer of dust off the cover, then wiped it with her thumb. With its soft, brown leather cover, at first glance it looked like a bible, but when she opened it and rifled through she realised it was a children's book. Judging by the illustrations and title of the book, it appeared to be aimed at younger readers.

"The battle of the Oak King and the Holly King," she read aloud. She raised her eyes to the attic. "Is this your book, Jimbo?"

No response. Aisling ran her fingers across the soft leather then brought it to her nose and sniffed, closing her eyes to enjoy the visceral sensation of the book. She imagined Jimbo touching it a century before and the thought gave her an idea; she flipped to the page after the title and scanned for a publication date.

1895.

Did that mean Jimbo lived in the late 1800s? Mind you, the book could have been old even during his lifetime, especially if it was passed down through a generation. Books often were back then, when they held more sentimental appeal than the mass produced paperbacks of modern society. Aisling thought to a copy of *A Child's Garden of Verses* by Robert Louis Stevenson that her grandmother had gifted to her when she had been eight years old; the same age as she had been when she had received it in her own childhood. Was this book a childhood present that Jimbo had received when he had been a boy? Imagining the possibilities about his life made her feel closer to him; Aisling hugged the book close to her chest then took it downstairs to read with a final word over her shoulder. "Thank you Jimbo. I promise I'll take good care of it."

Good excuse for a cuppa. Aisling made the tea and loaded several chocolate digestives onto a saucer, then sat at the small kitchen table and spread the book open.

Once upon a time there was a majestic King who lived in the forest. He had skin as green as summer grass and wore a crown of oak leaves upon his brow. His regal clothes were fashioned from the fresh spring leaves, made by the elves and sprites of the forest themselves. When he rode his golden chariot through the glorious spring forest, every flower, plant and tree in full leaf would bow its head and rain a carpet of petals before him, to serenade his coming.

Aisling paused to sip her tea and take a bit of chocolate biscuit. This was clearly the Oak King of Scandinavian folklore; she thought back to another childhood book that she had owned, with a story about *Sir Gawain and the Green Knight*, the latter another character who had been based on the mythology of the Oak King.

Everywhere he went, the majestic King of Summer made sure that each leaf he touched raised its pristine green splendour to the sun and every flower spread its petals wide to the sky. His kingdom was a midsummer majesty to behold! But as the days grew shorter and the colours changed from green to brown, red and orange, the oak leaves of his crown began to wilt and the King began to droop his head. His strength was waning.

Another sip of tea and bite of biscuit. Despite being a children's book, Aisling felt herself immersed in the story.

There was talk of another King on the move. A King who wore a crown of holly leaves and berries with a fine, white beard that sat on his chest in a thick braid. A king who wore a long cloak of deep green leather, with a white trim of the finest arctic fox fur. He rode on a sleigh of silver, pulled across the snows by four proud stags. Everything he touched with his tall, white birch-wood staff became coated with the most glorious, shimmering sheen of ice, or dusting of frost. He was ready for the battle of Midsummer.

This was exciting; never mind kids, Aisling was gripped.

But the birch-wood staff was powerful, bringing blow upon blow to the golden chariot and crown of oak leaves. The King of

Summer was defeated. His crown fell to the forest floor and the oak leaves became as golden-brown as the coming harvest. Night became longer and days became shorter in celebration of the King of Winter taking the throne in his winter wonderland. Trees, once in full leaf became red, brown and orange and flowers, once in full bloom, wilted and folded their petals for another year.

Aisling studied the illustration of the Oak King's defeat by the Holly King showing him slinking away into the forest, biding his time for another half year.

Everywhere, cold wind blew and snow flurries spread across the land. The King of Winter reigned supreme. But, just as he had come forth and conquered, so too did he feel the approach of the King of Summer. The King of Summer had been quietly resting and gathering his strength. Now he was ready to fight again, prepared for the Battle of Midwinter. Wielding his sword and shield of oak, he sprang a surprise attack on the King of Winter. His sword was strong, splintering the birch-wood staff. His golden chariot was fast, dazzling the stags that pulled the silver sleigh. He defeated the King of Winter and brought with him the return of light to the world.

Aisling closed the book. It was an interesting story of the solstices and seasonal change in the world. But why did Jimbo have it in the attic, and why did he choose to show it to her?

Chapter five

*L*ast Christmas I gave you my heart blared across the living room at a level that was loud enough to reach the kitchen, and maybe out into the hallway, but hopefully wouldn't disturb the neighbours. Mind you, the neighbours on either side were also students, so Aisling doubted they would care too much in any case. Eleven people from her History with Irish course had arrived; a small number by most people's standards, but Aisling was pleased. Maybe she did have some friends after all.

As she carried a tray of eggnog walnut snowballs into the living room, Aisling's eyes travelled around her guests, then stopped on Liv. She had made much effort for the party, looking very glam in a short, red, sequinned dress with long sleeves that suited her trim, curvy figure. Aisling felt both jealous of being upstaged at her own party and flattered that Liv considered her party important enough to have gone the extra mile; she really wanted friends and more than anything to fit in. Aisling glanced down at her own outfit; a shapeless Christmas jumper with a cartoonlike Rudolph reindeer on the front and her long, dark hair bunched on either side like reindeer ears to match the antler hairband she was wearing. Next to Liv, she looked – and felt – childish. Not a comforting thought; she dragged her gaze away from Liv and zoned in on Eoin. His choice of outfit made her feel less self-conscious: he had chosen a tacky Christmas t-shirt reading *Io Saturnalia*, fitting for a History student in Aisling's opinion, but underneath was a cartoonish snowman wearing a sun crown as *King for a Day*.

Aisling smiled as she approached him. "Cool t-shirt."

Eoin gave a nod to her jumper. "Yours too. Very festive."

His eyes lingered on her chest and she blushed, before realising that he was looking at Rudolph's face and not her boobs. He gave her a broad smile, his eyes crinkling, and the heat returned to her face; maybe he *was* indeed checking her out.

A thud coming from the stairwell diverted her thoughts from Eoin. Friends in the real world and friends in the other world too. Aisling walked into the hallway and glanced up the stairs at the fairy lights. The battery case had slipped off the bannister, dangling between the plug in its socket and the multi-coloured fairy lights. It had banged against the wooden handrail, explaining the thud she had heard. She climbed a few steps and reattached it using the piece of duct tape dangling from the bannister above. Strange that the strong tape hadn't secured it. Had Jimbo released it on purpose to get her attention?

In the past week since she had seen Jimbo through the mirror, Aisling hadn't tried to make any further contact with him. She sensed, however, that although the energy in her house was cold, it was friendly and not sinister. When Jimbo had appeared behind her, he had been grinning. She recalled his smiling face now; at the time, she had knocked herself out with the shock – both of falling down the stairs and of seeing his ghost – but now, she felt more intrigued than afraid. Jimbo hadn't been an old person, as she had been imagining when she thought of a stereotypical ghost. Quite the contrary in fact; he had the dancing eyes and a youthful smile. What had killed a young man, in the prime of his life, a century ago?

Aisling stole away from her party, leaving her guests drinking and mingling in the living room. An idea popped to mind; she took a sprig of mistletoe from the wreath on her front door and closed her fingers around it. She climbed the stairs to the landing, leaning on the newel post after one too many Baileys, and looked up at the attic hatch.

"Jimbo? Are you there?"

Aisling watched the attic hatch, but it remained closed.

It wasn't the first time that week that she had been left feeling stupid. What would it look like if one of her friends walked out of the living room and caught her, talking to thin air? She would lose all her new companions, and not only that; they would spread word of her being a looney too.

In answer, the fairy lights on the stairwell flickered. Darkness seemed to concentrate on the landing, as though grey-black smoke had poured from the attic and began to materialise into a human silhouette. Aisling watched the dark mass of ethereal shadow condense into a figure with broad shoulders that stood around six feet tall.

"Merry Christmas, Jimbo." Aisling extended her arm towards the shadow, holding a sprig of mistletoe between them, above the height of the shadow figure's head.

The ghost moved closer, and in the gloom, she could distinguish the same soulful eyes and smiling mouth she had glimpsed before. This time in addition, she could discern a straight, pointed nose and chiselled jawline among the grey-black shadow face. As Jimbo's dark, shadowy mass closed the distance between them, Aisling felt a tingling sensation touch her lips; a jolt of static electricity. Aisling likened the feeling to the time when she had taken a mild allergic reaction to a menthol lip-balm; painful, but not without a strange, soothing pleasure.

Had Jimbo responded to her Christmas greeting? Yes. She had received her first kiss from a spirit.

"I get it now, Jimbo. This is your house, and as tempted as you were to haunt me, you like me too much."

Aisling couldn't say how she could sense it, but she knew she was on the right track, though he didn't speak.

"You're lonely like me, and you've grown rather found of me since I moved in."

Again, she knew she was right, and continued.

"My fairy lights attracted you as the electrical charge brings this world – and the other world – close together. It's like a lightning rod. That's how you were able to physically move the switch."

Right again. She knew it and so did Jimbo. The shadow-ghost before her was listening.

"I've decided I won't try to remove you from my house. It was my intention to exorcise you at first. But now I quite like you." A blush crept over her cheeks. "I'll let you stay, provided we can get to know each other better – and also that you never sneak up on me when I'm not expecting it."

Ground rules accepted; Aisling sensed it.

"Well, that's all then. Merry Christmas Jimbo."

Aisling kept her arm raised, holding the white berries over their heads. As the shadow form engulfed her, Aisling closed her eyes and pouted her lips, ready for another spirit kiss. In her mind she heard a reply to her greeting: *Merry Christmas, Aisling.* Though the ghost never said a word.

Chapter six

After her first ghost-kiss, Aisling had spent the rest of her party the previous evening dancing and mingling with her guests in an enchanted delirium. All thoughts of having friends, or no friends, had gone out of her head; she could easily have spent last night alone in her house with Jimbo and not felt lonely. That aside, she was glad her friend Liv had fallen asleep in the spare room after one too many drinks, as it was good to have someone living to share her news with.

"I've got to ask you a question. Do you believe in ghosts?" said Aisling.

Liv raised her eyebrows. "I've never seen one. But I'm interested in the idea of them. Why?"

"Did I tell you there's a ghost in this house?" said Aisling.

Liv blinked at her as if she had spoken another language.

"It started with my fairy lights malfunctioning. There's a lot of spiritual energy in this house and that's how I contacted him the other night. The fairy lights were blinking every time I asked him a question."

Liv looked like she had swallowed a sour plum. "You're saying, you spoke to a ghost that lives in this house?"

Aisling nodded. "Not only that, I saw him too. He's a young man. He was attractive when he was alive."

Spit flew at Aisling as Liv cackled, throwing her head back.

"I'm being serious," said Aisling, wiping saliva off her cheek.

"You seriously need a shag," Liv gasped.

Liv could really be annoying, but she would be convinced soon. "He gave me a book, did you know? It fell out of the attic hatch, where I saw his face peering at me. This is the book, if you want proof that these things are actually happening."

Aisling handed *The Battle of the Oak King and Holly King* to her. Liv turned the book over in her hands, examining it. Her long eyelashes swept from side to side as she devoured the words on the first page and a pale blonde coil of hair sprung forward onto her cheek. Aisling gulped watching her. Did Liv believe her?

Liv looked up from the book, her kohl-ringed eyes half shut. Was she bored? Tired? Whatever the reaction, Aisling started to feel irritated. "Seriously, you're saying that basically, there's a ghost haunting your house?"

Aisling balled, then unballed her fists, trying to control her annoyance. "Yes, that's what I've been trying to tell you. Have you got wax in your ears, or what?"

Liv ran her thumb across the edges of the pages, flicking them really fast, then chucked the book onto the sofa. "So what? This says nothing. It's just an old book. What do you expect in a house that's about a hundred years old? It doesn't mean there's a ghost here, or nothing."

How could she prove her point to such a staunch disbeliever? Aisling shook her head, casting a curtain of dark brown hair around her face.

Liv extended a finger and pushed Aisling's hair back off her cheek, tucking it behind her ear. "You know, you're so cute when you get upset, you silly girl."

Aisling turned and faced Liv, square on, on the sofa. "Are you saying you believe me?"

"I didn't say that." Liv smiled. "But if there really is a ghost, and he really gave you this book, why didn't you tell me about it sooner?"

Aisling pondered Liv's question and her answer. Why not, indeed?

"Well, it only happened a few days ago and I needed to think about what it meant – why he gave it to me." Aisling shrugged. "Besides, if I'd told you yesterday at my Christmas party, you would have cleared out of the house. Everyone would have. Who would want to stay in a house that's haunted?"

"Are you kidding? That would've made your party *way* more exciting – not that it wasn't already fun." Liv winked at Aisling. "No offence intended. But if you'd said something, we all could've gone up there into the attic on a ghost hunt."

Aisling wrinkled her nose and sank back into the sofa.

Liv jumped to her feet and held her hand out to Aisling. "In fact, why don't we go up there now, you and I? Have you got a ladder?"

She shook her head. In a way, Aisling was glad that she didn't have a ladder; it seemed like an insult to Jimbo to treat him like a curiosity, rather than a human being, who had once had a life. He might be a ghost, but he was still a person.

Liv flopped back down onto the sofa beside Aisling. After a moment of pouting, she sat up with a dazzling smile of perfect white teeth. "I know – I've got it. A Newton's Cradle."

"A what?" said Aisling.

"It's a pendulum made of ball bearings. My flat mate is a Physicist, so that's how I know. It's these five metal balls on wires, you see. You lift one at the end and when it swings down and hits the others, the one on the end flies up. It goes on like this for ages," said Liv.

"Oh yeah, I know what you're talking about, I saw one a long time ago. But what have they got to do with anything?"

Liv jiggled with excitement, her blonde curly hair bouncing. "Well, apparently the Law of Conservation of Energy states that energy can neither be created nor destroyed, it can only be converted from one form into another."

So what was the punchline. "Yeah, and?" said Aisling.

"And what are ghosts, but pure energy. Think about it. They're spirits. They exist in a dimension of electrical energy, or at least a highly charged state, don't they?"

Aisling understood; they could contact Jimbo by using a Newton's Cradle. "I get it. But where do we get one?"

Liv jumped to her feet with a squeal and a jiggle. "Lisa, my flat mate has one. Oh, this is so exciting! I'll go get it now. Wait right here. Be right back!"

Aisling watched her fly out of the house in a flurry of blonde curls and shimmering red party dress. Once her friend had left the house, she raised her eyes to the ceiling. "Jimbo, if you're up there listening, I hope we aren't going to be disturbing your sleep. Liv's a bit full-on, but she's a nice girl and her heart's in the right place.

Aisling tucked her legs up on the sofa, curling into a foetal ball for comfort as she mused about what the Newton's Cradle would uncover. It felt less intrusive than physically going up into the attic to root around in Jimbo's domain. Would the ball bearings make a stronger connection than the layman's mirror-séance she had tried at the top of the stairs? She had tried the mirror-séance one time since the first try, and it hadn't worked; in her opinion, any other method to try and make contact with Jimbo was worth a go.

She heard the front door open a half hour later and Liv swept into the living room, her face flushed from hurrying. "Let's go upstairs, I've got it here."

Aisling saw the Newton's Cradle that she held in her outstretched hand. "Alright, I'm thinking we try the landing again, right under the attic hatch."

They hurried upstairs. Aisling used the tip of her large golf umbrella to slide the attic hatch fully open; she was sure if Jimbo were to appear, he would show himself in the darkness above as he had before. Liv sat cross-legged on the floor with the Newton's Cradle in front of her and Aisling sat opposite her in the same position with their knees touching, so that they enclosed it between them. From their seated position in the middle of the landing, below the attic hatch, Aisling had a good view of the bathroom ahead. The mirror hanging on the wall where the top of the stairs turned onto the landing showed her a view of the master bedroom behind. Aisling caught sight of her own reflection and fixed a stray hair sticking up; if Jimbo were to appear, she wanted to look her best.

Liv lifted one of the ball bearings and let it go, causing it to swing downwards and strike the next in line with a click. The ball bearing on the opposite end swung up, then down causing the ball bearings on both ends to seesaw up and down in turn. Aisling took hold of Liv's hands and held them in her own; they were soft and warm. Liv smiled at her, and Aisling felt a warm surge in her face.

"Jimbo, are you here with us today?" said Aisling.

A cold breeze prickled the back of her neck. Aisling gasped, then exhaled the air she had sucked into her chest slowly, soothing herself.

"I sense that you're here – that you've always been here. But I'd like to see you. Could you show yourself to us?" She looked up at the attic hatch, but no smiling face appeared.

"Maybe he isn't in the house today?" said Liv, the excitement on her face waning.

"Where else would he go, he lives here," Aisling said with a shrug.

Liv tilted her head to either side in a gesture that Aisling took as accepting her explanation. Aisling cleared her throat and went on. "You gave me your book – the children's story of the Oak King and the Holly King? What is it you want to tell me?"

Liv gasped and pointed at Aisling. "Oh my gosh, your hair."

Aisling felt the tingle of static electricity tickling her cheeks. A glance at her reflection showed her long, dark hair standing upright in all directions. She looked at Liv. Her blonde curls began to rise upwards off her head.

"He's near," said Aisling, her voice hoarse. She swallowed to wet her dry throat. "I can feel him."

Aisling looked again at the mirror. Standing behind her, in the doorway of the master bedroom, was the grey-black vapourish mass she had seen twice before. Aisling could see the outline of Jimbo's face, clearer in broad daylight than the previous evening. He had floppy hair that fell forward on his forehead, though she couldn't tell what colour it would have been in life. His deep-set, soulful eyes were smiling as he watched her in the mirror. He had a short beard and moustache, but like his hair, she couldn't tell what colour they would have been when he was alive. He had angular cheekbones and a chiselled jawline beneath the short beard. Jimbo would most certainly have been a *looker* when he had been alive. His presence was so *physical* that it took a moment for her to remember he was dead. The thought jolted her back to reality with a start.

"Liv, he's behind me. Can you see him?" Her voice came out as barely more than a whisper.

Liv's eyes darted back and forth as she searched behind Aisling. "Where?"

Aisling pressed her lips together in frustration.

"I'm not seeing anything." She rose up onto her knees to look over Aisling.

Liv's eyes widened and with a shriek, she fell forwards into Aisling's arms. "I saw something – there was a shadow, further back, near the wardrobe."

Aisling pushed Liv away and searched her face. Did she really see Jimbo, or was she going along with the moment? It was so hard to say.

A crack and splintering noise jerked her from her thoughts. Both Aisling and Liv turned and looked in the direction of the bathroom. The mirror had been smashed.

Was Jimbo angry? But what could he be mad about?

Aisling's hair dropped back across her shoulders from where it had been standing erect, full of electrical discharge mere moments before. Liv's curls had also bounced back into place. The static electricity had vanished from her house.

"Jimbo? Have you gone?" said Aisling.

A cheeky smirk spread across Liv's face. "Maybe he's jealous. He doesn't like you having a new friend."

"I doubt that could be the case, as this is only the third time I've seen him, so I'd hardly call us friends." Aisling looked down at the ball bearings. She grabbed the one nearest to her when it swung upwards and stopped the rhythm. Thoughts of her ghostly kiss with him the previous evening flitted to mind. "Maybe he doesn't like me after all."

Chapter seven

"**O**h my goodness, did you hear?"

"Yeah, I know. She thinks there's a ghost in her house."

"I know. Apparently she even contacted it through her mirror. She thinks that they're seeing each other."

"She must be, like, *majorly* crazy."

"Oh, shut up. Here she comes."

Aisling's heart sank as she approached her classmates; two who had been at her party only two days before on Saturday night. Their red faces and guilty expressions did nothing to assuage the hurt she felt. Not at the gossip, not even at the fact that they thought she was nuts. No; she was hurt because it was obvious who had told them. Liv had stabbed her in the back.

Liv. Aisling puffed out her cheeks then blew out the air. So much for having a new friend; and she had seemed so keen on making contact with Jimbo too. Aisling thought of how her so-called friend had jiggled with excitement at the thought of using the Newton's Cradle, how she had seemed to believe Aisling about contacting his ghost through the mirror. The mirror that was now broken, because Jimbo felt betrayed – or so it seemed. Aisling had no friends in the real world, or the other world either, for that matter. Loneliness smacked her like a tidal wave of solid bricks, right in her gut.

Speak of the Devil. Liv walked into the lecture theatre, her scarf flapping behind her and blonde coils bouncing. She caught Aisling's eye, slipped her an awkward smile then dropped her gaze and hurried on towards the front of class. Aisling felt a prickle in each eye. As their professor talked, she barely heard the lecture on Ancient Egypt during the Ptolemaic period, hardly took any notes. Instead, her fingers were pressed into the corner of each eye to stop the tears flowing. Why was she so different and weird; why couldn't she make friends easily? She seemed to alienate everyone who got to know her and she didn't know why.

***

Another eggnog. Heat seared through Aisling's cheeks and stung her hairline. She wiped her fringe back off her forehead and took another sip. Her head was beginning to spin. She wasn't normally a drinker, the bottle had been a leftover from the eggnog walnut snowballs she had made for her party on Saturday, but she needed the alcohol. She had a serious case of Monday blues. Forget that; sad-sack syndrome. Liv had seemed like the sort of outgoing, bubbly person that would have been perfect to draw in a new circle of friends. Now she was back to having nothing. Anti-nothing; all the guests who had attended her party thought she was nuts, which was worse than being a nobody. Judging by the cracked mirror on her landing, she didn't have Jimbo's friendship either.

She needed to get a grip on herself. If her classmates thought she was nuts, then they weren't friends at all. Who needed friends like that? Aisling hauled herself off the sofa and went through to the kitchen. Feeling sorry for herself got her nowhere. She would pull herself together and the first step was sobering up. Coffee. The second step would be to clear the air with Liv, to ask her why she spread rumours to their classmates. The third step would be to find, and make amends, with Jimbo.

Aisling filled the kettle and clicked the switch. A loud zap preceded a sting at the tips of her fingers.

"Aow!" She shook her hand to dispel the pain from the electric shock.

"She wasn't worth it," said a whisper.

Aisling turned and looked back through to the living room. "Jimbo?"

"Take more care with the people you invite into this house," said the whisper.

It had to be Jimbo. But how was she able to hear him? He hadn't spoken at all so far. Aisling abandoned the kettle and her eggnog on the kitchen counter and followed the direction of the whisper.

"Jimbo? Where are you?"

"You know the answer to that," said the whisper.

Aisling followed the voice upstairs. A tingle travelled from the crown of her head to her feet and she padded across the landing at a quicker pace, despite her tipsiness. A rope ladder hung from the open hatch of the attic. It had a dusty, aged appearance, but looked to be sturdy. She hesitated before stepping onto the first rung, then took the leap into the ether.

Darkness. Aisling let her eyes adjust to the gloom. She could see Jimbo's tall silhouette outlined by dancing particles of dust that reflected light from below through the open hatch. As the condensed dark shadow approached, Aisling saw that his form appeared even more solid today than he had previously been, like black ink poured into water.

"Are you really a ghost?" she asked. "You seem more dense today – I can see you clearer than before."

"This is the only form I have that can travel between the worlds," said Jimbo. His voice spoke in her head, a whisper that her mind made real; not an actual voice with depth and body like that of a physical person. "The connection between my world and this house is getting stronger."

Aisling extended a finger towards the dark phantasm, but felt nothing. Not even coldness; nothing.

"I thought you would be solid. You know, made of ectoplasm, or something else I could touch," she said, her voice sounding sad as it reached her own ears. "You touched me two days ago. You kissed me, at my party on Saturday."

"Electrical discharge, nothing more."

She shook her head. "Then why don't I get any electrical shock when I try to touch you now?"

"You must be numb from the shock that machine gave you," said Jimbo, in a whisper, in her mind.

Machine? What shock? She thought of downstairs in her kitchen moments before. "Oh, you mean when my kettle electrocuted me."

"You need to be careful," said Jimbo. "You don't want to end up in this place where I am. Take care not to get injured again."

His words caused her to massage her own fingertips in a protective gesture, even though they no longer throbbed after the electric shock. "I'll try. Though being honest, you've given me hope. I'm not afraid of dying now that I've met you. It's good to know there's a world beyond our own – and you're proof."

Aisling's thoughts lurched to her mum. Mum had died when she was eight. Dad would love it if she could make contact with her mum, let him know that–

"There are many worlds, and the one that I'm in isn't heaven. Trust me when I say that you don't want to end up in this existence. Many people have lived in this house before you, but the connection between us must be strong as you're the first I've spoken to. The first who has seen me. I ask you to stay away from me. Don't try to contact me again. It's for your own good. Keep away from your acquaintance, Liv. That implement she brought into this house is dangerous."

"Dangerous?" The word had barely left Aisling's lips when a bright flash from the landing below stole her attention away from Jimbo. The fairy lights had lit up as though a thousand volts had flooded the circuit. She winced, shielding her eyes with her arms, and when she turned back to where Jimbo had stood, he was gone.

Aisling climbed back down the rope ladder onto the landing below. Talking to Jimbo had left her completely sober. Why didn't he want her to contact him anymore? What harm could come to her from communicating with the other world?

Instead of going back downstairs, Aisling turned and went into her bedroom. The Newton's Cradle from Liv's house mate sat benignly on her bedside table. What was so dangerous about five ball bearings suspended by strips of wire?

Chapter eight

Yuletide. Aisling popped open Day 21 on her advent calendar and ate the chocolate snowman inside. During the past week at her lectures and tutorial classes, she had managed to avoid speaking to Liv, or even making eye contact with her, but it wasn't because Liv had betrayed her. It was because of Jimbo.

She still didn't know what to make of Jimbo's warning. If he thought the Newton's Cradle was dangerous, then why didn't he simply ask her to remove it from the house? He had said to keep away from Liv herself. Was it a combination of Liv and the Newton's Cradle that was dangerous? Or could it be that Liv was the danger, and had a bad influence on the ball bearings?

It hadn't helped that Jimbo was as good as his word and refused to be contacted. Aisling had tried to use the combination of fairy lights and mirror as she had the first time she'd made contact with him – to no avail. She had then tried linking her hands around the Newton's Cradle and beseeching him to talk to her – without actually starting the ball bearings in motion – again wasting her efforts. It seemed that Jimbo had wandered off into the limbo world where he resided and was either ignoring Aisling, or was unwilling to let their connection draw him near her.

Tomorrow she would be going home to her dad and brother for Christmas, and soon she would be absorbed in the usual huge family affair with all their aunts, uncles, cousins, nieces and nephews and Jimbo would be gone from her mind. Today she could think of nothing else. Yet the house was as an empty shell. She resented it, maybe unfairly, but either way had to get outside. Yes, a walk would clear her head.

Aisling pulled on her coat, boots and hat. It was tempting to jump in the car and go for a drive to air her feelings, but the lure of local haunts tugged at her more and so she let her feet dictate the way.

Soft snowflakes began to fall as she walked past the Welcome Chinese restaurant and the Jeggy Nettle Pub on Stranmillis Road. Maybe it would be a white Christmas for the first time since she could remember. Aisling was so busy looking upwards, watching the white flurry fall from an endless white ocean of clouds, that she didn't notice where her feet had taken her until she arrived at the large, gothic gates of Friar's Bush Graveyard, set within the high, stone walls.

Aisling pushed her face between the bars and stared into the graveyard. She didn't know much about it, except that it was Belfast's oldest Christian burial ground, said to have been established by St. Patrick, Patron Saint of Ireland himself.

A gasp escaped her as the wrought iron gate jerked forward, making Aisling stumble. It was unlocked. Did that mean the graveyard was open for visitors? Or could it be that the groundskeeper – if there was one – had accidently left it unlocked?

She pushed the gate open further, hearing the metallic groan of the hinges, and took a cautious step inside. Her foot resting on the cobbled ground. "Hello? Are you open to the public?"

No reply. Aisling tried the wooden door to her right then across to the one facing it on the left. Both were locked. That meant there was no groundskeeper in the vicinity. She closed the gate behind her, making it look like it was locked and hoped that nobody else would wander off the street behind her. It wouldn't be good if she were to be blamed for causing trespassers, not knowing if she was uninvited herself. It wasn't the main reason she wanted to explore the graveyard incognito; she wanted to do this alone. Her subconscious had led her there for a reason, maybe even a supernatural influence; she needed to find out why.

The short grassy path ahead took Aisling on a straight route between the gravestones. Her knowledge of Friar's Bush Graveyard was limited; they buried plague victims in mass graves, she knew that, and they held secret mass for Catholics when Penal Laws against Catholicism were introduced in the 1600s.

Aisling made an abrupt halt in the middle of the graveyard. An unruly bush, its tangled limbs jutting out in all directions attracted her attention.

"The Maytree always gets people's attention."

Startled by the voice behind her, Aisling spun around. A young woman that Aisling guessed was around her own age stood smiling at her. Her pale skin was moon-bright and she had long, beige-brown hair that in the snowy, overcast sky glimmered with a silvery hue. Her wide, catlike eyes were yellowish green, as vivid as the lichen on the tombstones. The unusual shade gave them a penetrating power, almost as though the woman could see into her soul. Aisling felt a jolt in the pit of her stomach as the woman stared at her. She had a dazzling beauty that Aisling had never encountered before in a real person; she found herself stunned into submission at the woman's presence.

"It'll gift you a few of its Pixie Pears, if you like. They reduce blood pressure. I can tell that your heart is racing," the woman continued.

Aisling's hand leapt to her chest. The woman was right; her heart indeed raced. She took a deep breath to calm herself and tore her eyes away from the woman's face, so she could compose herself.

"Pixie Pears?" Aisling's voice was choked. She cleared her throat to wet it. "You mean the berries?"

The woman nodded. "The Maytree doesn't gift its precious fruit to just anyone. You need to be very special for it to bestow its gift upon you."

"Who are you?" Aisling straightened her pose into a more authoritative stance. Who was this strange woman making her feel awkward and uncomfortable?

"My name is Cliona," she said, in a velvety voice that matched her mesmorising form.

Aisling gulped and looked away again, this time towards the Maytree. She focused on it to distract herself from the woman's powerful aura. Could she be another ghost, this person, just like Jimbo? No real woman could ever make Aisling feel so odd and unsettled, the way Cliona did. "Cliona. That's a beautiful name. Unusual."

Cliona ignored Aisling's compliment, a mischievous smile on her face. She disappeared within the twisted, thorny boughs of the Maytree and a soft, whispering floated in the still air as the branches rustled. The strange woman emerged with two handfuls she had taken from the hawthorn tree and opened her palms to show Aisling the contents of each. Her right hand held red berries, similar to those of holly, and her left hand carried a handful of white blossoms.

Aisling looked back at the Maytree. Its branches were bare, as she expected in late December. No leaves, and certainly no flowers or fruit. Dread filled her. This woman couldn't be a ghost; she had more power than that. She took a step back from Cliona. "How did you do that? Where did you get those flowers and berries?"

"Don't be afraid. I'm trying to show you the power of the Maytree. It isn't me – it's the force coming from the hawthorn." Cliona stretched her hands out and Aisling found herself reaching for the contents of each, unable to resist the spell the strange beauty held. She cupped her hands around the berries and flowers.

"Why are you giving me these?"

"As I've already told you, the berries reduce blood pressure. The flowers can be made into a sedative. If you boil them together and strain them, they will make a pleasant tea. Drink it."

"Who are you?" Aisling repeated. "Why do you want me to make a tea out of these?"

"They'll help you. They'll put you into a suitable state to get the answers you need," said Cliona.

"What answers?" she said, her voice full of suspicion.

Cliona chortled. "You want to know more about Jimbo, don't you?"

Aisling studied the contents of each hand. What if the berries were poison? She was so distracted by thoughts of brewing hawthorn tea that it took a moment for her brain to catch up to what Cliona said. Aisling snapped out of her thoughts and looked up.

"How do you know about Jimbo?"

But her voice floated into the emptiness of Friar's Bush Graveyard. Cliona had gone.

Gone? Or disappeared? Maybe the strange woman was a ghost after all. How else could she have vanished into thin air? How else could she have known about Jimbo? How else could she have conjured flowers and berries of summer right on the midwinter solstice? Aisling felt disturbed; Yuletide had turned out to hold more supernatural power than she could ever have envisaged.

Chapter nine

What on earth was she doing? Aisling looked at the strained mush of hawthorn flower petals and dissolved berries that she had dumped in her sink. It was crazy to follow the instructions of a mysterious, paranormal woman that she had met, not an hour before, in a centuries old deserted graveyard. When she put it that way to herself, it sounded like a demented notion that only a moron would follow.

If she hadn't already made contact with the ghost of Jimbo, she never would have believed such absurd advice.

Yet there she stood, at the kitchen sink, about to drink 'Pixie Pear' tea. Aisling looked at the pale-yellow drink with tiny fragments of leaf litter and berry skin sediment at the bottom. She raised the mug to her nose and sniffed. No smell. She touched the rim to her lips and took the tiniest sip; no taste.

A bland, odourless poison to make her into a ghost just like Jimbo. Maybe that was how she would meet him.

Aisling spluttered on the drink, spraying Pixie Pear tea all over her clean plates in the dish rack. No; she had to keep faith. This drink supposedly had a sedative effect. Was relaxation the key to finding out more about Jimbo? Probably if she sedated her physical self into a more malleable form, then she could become closer to the other world. Maybe her mind could enter the other world more easily, and therefore make seamless contact with Jimbo to find out more about him?

She would find out soon, at any rate. Bottoms up, she willed herself, and gulped down the hot tea in one go.

After a few minutes, a calm sleepiness took hold of her. Aisling walked across the living room to the large bay window overlooking her small front garden. She flopped into a chair, steadying herself with one hand on the arm rest. Her eyes roved the clutter that lined the window ledge: Jimbo's book, The battle of the Oak King and the Holly King; a bowl and spoon stained with red lipstick from her party the previous weekend; Liv's flatmate's Newton's Cradle and her golf umbrella with its handle propped up against the window. Each object sat in a line across the ledge. Her gaze jumped across them: book; bowl; ball-bearings; brolly, then veered upwards and out the window, settling on the holly bush at the end of her garden.

Book, bowl, ball-bearings, brolly, bush. Book, bowl, ball-bearings, brolly, bush. One, two, three, four, five.

The first four in a row, the fifth in a central position above them, forming a triangle between one and five. All starting with the letter 'B'. Was there a connection? Could there be a significance?

Book, bowl... Aisling's train of thought ground to a halt. She let her focus settled on the ball-bearings. Metal balls. Five metal balls, held in a pendulum. She shifted the Newton's Cradle sideways and studied it. A triangular pendulum. Five 'b's within a triangular pendulum.

Coldness pooled in Aisling's stomach. This was more than coincidence.

She pushed the other objects aside, clearing space on either side of the Newton's Cradle. Jimbo had told her not to use it and not to contact him again; she hadn't heard from him in a couple of days. She had respected his word and not tried it since then, even when she had linked her hands around it to make a circle with her arms, in an effort to contact him; she hadn't actually set the balls in motion. Now she stared at the stationary balls in front of her. Jimbo didn't want her to use the Newton's Cradle because it was effective, not dangerous; she was convinced. Starting the motion of the ball bearings would force him out of whatever limbo he resided in and compel him to make contact with her.

So be it. Aisling took a deep breath and pinched the ball bearing on the right side between her thumb and forefinger. She pulled it upwards and let go. The ball swung downwards and hit the one next to it on the left with a click. The fifth ball on the left side swung upwards in response. Aisling watched them and waited.

"Jimbo? I need to speak to you. Can you make contact, please?"

There was a notch of panic in her voice, a touch of desperation. Was she really so eager to see Jimbo? It wasn't as though he were alive; he had been dead at least a hundred years. She breathed in through her nose and out through her mouth, calming herself and watched the reflection in the large bay window, should he appear behind her.

Aisling glanced at her phone screen. Five minutes had passed and Jimbo hadn't made his presence known. Whether he was mad at her and avoiding her or not, she should have seen or heard something from him by now – if he were nearby. Maybe she was going about it the wrong way. She caught the ball bearing on the right side mid-swing and stopped it, then set it back in place.

The fairy lights popped into her mind. Could that be the missing part of the equation? Throughout all the supernatural occurrences in her house so far, they had always been switched on. Aisling slipped out of the living room and up the stairs to flick the switch.

She resumed her seat by the bay window and looked again at the inanimate ball bearings, then outside to the holly bush as she willed her subconscious to unleash any hidden knowledge it may have held. Nothing. Aisling rested both elbows on the window sill with a sigh, but as she did so her left elbow brushed the ball bearings, pushing the two leftmost upwards. They swung downwards together and struck the middle ball, which remained motionless; the two balls on the right side swung upwards in turn and down, setting a different rhythm in motion.

Jimbo's dark, shadowy figure materialised in the middle of the holly bush in Aisling's line of perspective behind the middle, stationary ball bearing. She yelped at his sudden appearance.

"I warned you, it's dangerous to contact me. You shouldn't get too close to the Netherworld where I am." His voice was a faint whisper, a telepathic message in her mind.

His wavering form glided across the garden in a straight line towards her and diffused through the bay window pane. Aisling tumbled backwards, knocking the armchair over and rolled head over heels onto her living room floor.

"If you don't want me to talk to you, I won't contact you again," she said.

Jimbo stopped moving towards her and floated on the spot, three feet from where she lay sprawled. "You know that isn't true."

Her heart sped up a notch. "Isn't true that you don't want me to talk to you, or isn't true that you don't want me to contact you again?" Aisling suppressed a smile; could Jimbo outsmart her quick thinking.

If ever a ghost could have blushed, she imagined Jimbo would have. "I want to contact you, and have you contact me, but I don't you to endanger yourself by our communication."

She sat up, cross-legged on the floor. "I'm not afraid of the other world."

"It isn't the other world, it's the Netherworld," came his quick reply, in her mind.

"Other world, Netherworld, I'm not scared of either." Aisling flapped her hands, as though to assuage her own fears. "I've been in contact with someone else from your world anyway. I met her earlier today at the cemetery around the corner."

"Cemetery? You mean Friar's Bush Graveyard?" Jimbo's raised his hands, warning her to stop. "Don't go there. That's where I died. It's where my body was lost."

So that's why she felt a spiritual energy pulling her feet towards Friar's Bush Graveyard; because Jimbo's body was buried in there somewhere. "But I want to find your gravestone, now that I know your body is in there."

"No, Aisling. Stay away from there, you hear? Promise me."

Her cheeks grew hot. "It would make me feel closer to you, if I know where your final resting place is. I want to see it."

He shook his head. "Don't go back there. Promise me."

She stared at his shadowy form, thinking fast. "It's probably too late. I drank a tea made of flowers and berries that I was given earlier today. I met a woman there."

"Pixie Pears. You met Cliona." Jimbo's neutral expression became angry. "I have to go. Please, Aisling. As much as I want to see you, you have to sever the connection with the Netherworld. Don't go back to Friar's Bush Graveyard and don't drink any more Hawthorn tea. I fear that what happened to me will happen to you. Switch off the fairy lights. You must not harbour strong energy in this house."

His dark figure began to fade.

"Pluck a sprig of holly and wear it on a necklace. If Cliona appears to you again, brandish it at her."

He was disappearing into the ether.

"Give the metal implement back to your acquaintance and have no more to do with the girl."

His shadowy form was almost gone, as though by osmosis.

"Wait," Aisling panted.

But she was alone.

Chapter ten

Aisling hauled her overnight bag out of the car and hurried into her house against the onslaught of rain. Christmas at home was always great as she got to spend quality time with dad and Naiose, but she felt socially burned out after the obligatory family gathering with Uncle Gerry over at his house in Finaghy. Since her grandparents had passed when she had been five, Uncle Gerry had always hosted a get-together on Boxing Day and as much as she liked her uncle, aunt and cousins, Aisling couldn't wait to get back to some solitude in her house for a few days, before the New Year's parties would start. Supposing she got invited, of course.

She kicked off her boots and slung her coat on the hook by the door. Unpacking could wait until later; when her mum had been alive, she had always done

Aisling's laundry during the Christmas break at home, but now that it was only her, dad and Naoise, things didn't get done like before. She would sort through her dirty clothes, and stuff that could be sprayed with a clothes refresher and worn again, another time. A tedious chore like that was a job for tomorrow.

A knock at her front door alerted Aisling before she even had the chance to sit. Couldn't be the post, could it? Looked like a man through the frosted glass of the front door; not very tall, with black hair.

Curious, Aisling swung the door open. Her classmate, Eoin, stood on the doorstep looking like a drowned rat.

"Season's greetings," he said, as rain dripped off his chin.

"Ack, look at you. Come in before you catch your death." Aisling chivvied him in and tugged at his jacket as he passed into the hall. She shook it off and hung it on the peg next to hers.

"I thought I'd pay you a visit. I wasn't sure if you'd gone back home for the whole two weeks or not," he said.

"Just Christmas and Boxing Day. My dad's house is only out in Glengormley, so it's easy to head back over if I feel lonely."

"Well, that's why I came, I guess." Eoin gave a wry smile. "I was a bit worried about you."

"About me? Don't be silly. What would you be worrying about me for?" Aisling pulled her face into what she hoped was a sceptical frown.

Eoin shrugged with one shoulder, trying to play nonchalant. "Stuff Liv had been saying to the others, that's all."

Aisling pushed past him into the living room with a sniff. "I'm over all that. What does Liv matter anyway? I've got other friends."

He followed her in and perched on the sofa armrest. "If it's any consolation, I believe you. About Jimbo, that is."

She folded her arms. The thought to press him on whether Liv had put him up to it crossed her mind, but she decided against. Maybe Eoin really did believe her, and was visiting her as part of a pity call. "So, you believe in ghosts, then?"

He nodded, though she noticed his eyebrows were raised, making his forehead wrinkle. "Mm-hmm. I saw my grandmother's ghost when I was five. She sat on the end of my bed and told me everything was okay just a few days after she died."

Aisling smiled and dropped her arms to her side. "Can I get you anything? Cup of tea, or a hot chocolate?"

"I'll take a green tea if you have any," he said.

Aisling busied herself in the kitchen and brought out a green tea for him and a chai for herself with chocolate sprinkles. "I thought I might be the only one back here. Stranmillis is empty, all the other students have gone home."

He cupped his hands around the mug and sipped the green tea she had made. "I'm like you. I prefer to go home for Christmas Day and stay until after Boxing Day then come back for my own head space. My family would put your head away, there's so many of them. I'm not religious anymore anyway, at least of Christianity; Saturnalia is more my holiday."

Aisling scoffed. "You really are like me then. I'm not practising myself, I do it just for dad. To be honest,

I don't like Christmas much. I busy myself with shopping and putting up lights, but it's all a distraction. I'm not sure what I believe in anymore. I definitely believe in the afterlife, but I'm not sure about the rest."

She sat on the sofa and Eoin slipped off the armrest onto the space next to her. They sipped their drinks in a comfortable silence. As much as she felt burnt out from all the social time with family, Aisling appreciated having Eoin's company, even if they didn't speak.

"Have you seen Jimbo much lately?" he said, after a time.

She scratched her head. "Yes and no. He's not willing to contact me. He wants me to stay away as he thinks I might put myself in some sort of danger if I get too close to his world."

"The spirit world?"

"He calls it the Netherworld. It's like he's stuck in purgatory, a limbo world," she said.

Eoin peered over the top of his glasses at her. "Jimbo is able to tell you all this? I mean like, he can talk to you, and all?"

She nodded. "It's not talking like you and I are doing right now. It's kind of like telepathy. I can hear him in my head. But his ghostly form – shadow apparition – whatever you want to call it, is becoming clearer each time he appears to me. It's as though the connection with his limbo world is getting stronger."

"Do you think there's actually a channel that he can pass through to see you – or that you could possibly pass through to see him?"

Aisling gawped at him. "Oh my gosh, Eoin. You genius! You've just given me the most incredible idea!"

She set her tea down on the floor and threw her arms around Eoin. Eoin's own tea splashed on his lap.

He gasped and set down his own mug. "What? What did I say?" His face was red, flustered at the praise.

"Jimbo is worried that I might come into the Netherworld. That's it. He's not worried about the energy between us pulling him into *this* world, the real world. He's worried I might end up *there*. That's why he kept going on about danger. Why didn't I see this before?" She jumped to her feet.

"What are you going to do?" said Eoin, standing too.

"The fairy lights. The electricity seems to cause a current between this world and the Netherworld. The ball bearings too–" She pointed at the Newton's Cradle. "They seem to harness the current and concentrate it. Now I'm thinking – what if we can use something that will channel all the electrical energy and open a portal, if you like, so that my spirit can go into the Netherworld."

Eoin's excitement faded; his face was pallid. "Why would you want your soul to go into the Netherworld?"

Aisling couldn't understand his apprehension. "Why not? Nobody has been there before, there could be so much we could learn."

He looked at her as if she were crazy. "I agree with Jimbo. It's sounds dangerous – and mad."

She ignored him. Her eyes were on the Newton's Cradle, still sitting on the bay window ledge where she had left it, overlooking the front garden. "Well, don't worry. I haven't found what I need to use as a channel for the electrical energy between the two worlds, so you can rest your mind. My spirit won't be going anywhere, anytime soon."

Eoin followed her line of sight. She watched his dark eyes skirting the objects lining her window sill. Instead of looking at the ball bearings, his gaze had landed on her golf umbrella, which was still propped up against the pane where she had left it.

Aisling looked from Eoin, to the brolly, and back to her friend. "Oh, Eoin. You really are on the ball today."

Overwhelmed with excitement at the solution before her, her umbrella in that very room, Aisling grabbed Eoin's face with both hands and kissed his forehead. Eoin pulled back from her, his glasses fogged with condensation. She saw his eyes flit from her left eye to her right as he studied her intentions then, misreading them, leaned forward and kissed her on the mouth.

Aisling jerked away from him as if she'd been stung by a wasp. She wiped her mouth with the back of her hand.

"Sorry." Eoin lowered his head into a submissive pose, watching his hands in his lap.

"It's alright. I think I may have given you the wrong message. I got really excited by what you told me, that's all. But I don't like you in that way – only as a friend," she said. "So I'm the one who's sorry – to you."

"You don't need to apologise. I'm used to it." He composed himself, sitting upright. "If it's any consolation, I actually like you as a friend too. But I thought you might've fancied me, and wanted to give you what I thought you wanted from me."

Aisling chuckled. "Is that really what you thought? You're too sweet. And you're a better friend than I'd imagined. I'm lucky I've got a friend like you – you make the first and only friend I've got."

He laughed too. "We're both weird together I suppose. You're the first friend I have as well."

Her laughter faded. "I don't want to take advantage of our friendship so soon, but I might as well ask. I wonder if you would help me try to get into the Netherworld using the golf umbrella with my fairy lights and the Newton's Cradle?"

Eoin looked sad. "I'm going to say no – but only because I worry that you might get electrocuted and die for real."

"Is that what you're worried about?" She touched his arm, trying to channel reassurance into him. "Then don't."

He shook his head. "I respectfully disagree. We're talking about things that we don't understand."

"Can we compromise then? If I figure out a way to do the experiment safely, and can assure you of that, then would you help me?"

He still looked dubious, but Aisling could see his shoulders slump as he relaxed. "Well, I'm no scientist. But I'd be lying if I said I wasn't a wee bit curious myself. If you can find out how to do it without actually killing either of us, then I'm in."

Chapter eleven

The holly necklace sitting on her collarbone didn't prickle Aisling as she had imagined it would have. She had fastened it by tying twine cord around the short stem that she had plucked from a small bunch in her garden. There was a cluster of five berries and two prickly leaves on the bunch. Jimbo hadn't specified whether she needed to include a certain number of leaves or berries for it to work; only that she needed to wear holly on a necklace and brandish it at Cliona, should she see her. What would passersby think if they saw her wearing it? They probably wouldn't give her a second glance; it was only three days after Christmas, so still within the season to wear holly, or mistletoe. Not that doing so was particularly common, but there was no point bothering about that. If Jimbo were to be believed, she needed to wear it for protection against Cliona.

She wasn't exactly following Jimbo's wishes anyway; she was on her way to Friar's Bush Graveyard to gather more hawthorn flower petals and berries to make another dose of Pixie Pear tea, so that she could get spiritually in tune with the Netherworld. Whether he liked it or not, she was determined to cross over and find him.

As before, the gate was unlocked and nobody else was about. It had to be more than coincidence. Yes, she was sure supernatural influences were keeping other people away and that Cliona was most likely behind this. Who was Cliona anyway? Jimbo hadn't said, but he had certainly been on edge when she had mentioned talking to her at Yuletide. Maybe she would find out more about Cliona too, once she passed over into the Netherworld.

With a glance behind both shoulders, just to double check that she was really alone, Aisling strode over to the bare branches of the hawthorn tree. Now that she stood in front of it, she felt silly. Had Cliona said an incantation before, or even simply a request for the Maytree to give her its flowers and fruit? Aisling had been so dazzled by Cliona at the time that she couldn't remember.

"Ahem," she said. "Maytree? I'd like to make some more Pixie Pear tea."

"Pixie Pear tea? That sounds interesting."

Aisling spun around, her heart in her throat. "Cliona?"

Not Cliona. Liv stood five feet behind her, both hands inside the pockets of a shaggy, pastel blue winter coat.

"Who's Cliona?"

Aisling glowered at her. "Nobody. I thought you were someone else, that's all."

Liv's cheeks were pink. "I sort of – um – followed you here. I was going to go to your house, but I saw you leaving, so I thought I'd try and catch you up."

"What do you want?" said Aisling, her voice cold.

Liv hung her head. "I wanted to say sorry for what I did. I'm not sure what made me do it."

"You strung me along. I wouldn't have invited you into my house to try and contact Jimbo if I thought you were only doing it to make fun of me."

"See that's the thing – I wasn't." Liv stretched a pleading hand towards Aisling, but Aisling made no move to accept it. "I believed you. I still do. But, I guess I was a bit afraid. The thing about you is that you aren't."

Liv trailed off. Her head was still lowered, but she raised her eyes to search Aisling's face.

"Aren't what?" Aisling made sure her voice sounded colder than ever; she had to rebuff Liv's apology, make sure she really meant it. What if it was another trick to spread more rumours?

"Aren't afraid to be different. Aren't afraid to try and contact a ghost, even if it makes other people think you're crazy. You believe in what you're doing. I guess I admire that." Liv's whole face flushed red. "I'd like to be a bit more like that myself, but I want people to like me. I'd rather fit in than be different."

"I'd rather be different than fake." Aisling turned away from Liv and faced the Maytree. Silence behind her gave her satisfaction; her words had stung Liv this time. Good. Liv should be sorry for spreading lies and turning their classmates against her. She had no time for gossipmongers.

"I like your necklace. Are you wearing it because of Jimbo's story – the one about the Oak King and the Holly King?"

Aisling rolled her eyes; Liv wasn't going to take the hint and leave, it seemed.

"Is that what this is – an oak tree? Is there some significance with Jimbo? Maybe that's why he showed you his book," said Liv.

The notion to tell Liv to leave was on the tip of her tongue, but as Aisling spun around to confront her, she paused as Liv's words sunk in. *Oak King. Holly King. Significance with Jimbo.*

Aisling's mouth dropped open. "Oh my God, why didn't I see the connection before? The seasons have something to do with this. That must have been what Jimbo was trying to tell me."

She touched the holly sprig suspended on rope around her neck and rolled her fingers around the berries while her mind raced. Jimbo had told her to brandish it against Cliona, should she appear.

"You mean, like holly for winter and oak for summer?" said Liv, cutting across Aisling's thoughts.

Aisling smiled at Liv; her former friend had redeemed herself. "Yes. He told me to wear holly on a necklace. I got this from a bush in my garden. It must be for protection."

Liv looked at the sprig around Aisling's neck. "That's kind of like how you're supposed to wear a garlic necklace to ward off vampires, isn't it? But who did Jimbo want you to ward off?"

"Cliona. She's not a woman. She's not a ghost either, as she doesn't appear like Jimbo does, as a shadow person. She's a supernatural being of some sort, though I don't know what."

"A demon, maybe?" Liv's eyes filled with excitement. "What if we brought her through into this world when we used the Newton's Cradle to make contact with Jimbo – you know, like how doing a séance can sometimes contact a malicious spirit instead of the person you want to talk to?"

Aisling shook her head. "She never appeared to me in my house. I first met her here, near this hawthorn tree, at Yuletide."

"Hawthorn. So let's say she has something to do with hawthorn and Jimbo has something to do with holly." Liv pulled out her phone, her eyes darting from side to side as she scanned the screen. "Let's see. Hawthorn is also known as the Maytree, or Maybush. The flowers have medicinal properties and can be used as a sedative and the berries, also known as Pixie Pears, have properties that reduce blood pressure."

Aisling looked back at the barren branches of the Maytree. "Cliona told me all this when I saw her at Yuletide. She somehow conjured hawthorn petals and berries, even on the Midwinter Solstice, and told me to make them into a tea, which I did."

Liv didn't take her eyes off her phone. "But did she mention that hawthorn is respected as a tree of enchantment under the protection of the fairy realms? It says here that if you sit under a hawthorn tree on the first of May, you might be whisked away for good to the fairy underworld."

Aisling's hand flew to her mouth. "You don't think that's what happened to Jimbo, do you? What if his body was taken into the Sidhe Realm, the fairy realm, on the first of May whenever he died a century ago?

Maybe that's what he meant when he told me about the shadow realm – it isn't the afterlife like heaven, where you go when you die. The Netherworld must be the Sidhe Realm."

"Do you think Cliona is one of the Sidhe then?" said Liv.

Could she be? What if Liv was right? Cliona certainly hadn't been a ghost, like Jimbo. She had radiated an ethereal energy, a supernatural presence that suggested she was an immortal being, but not like a soul or spirit that had once been alive as Jimbo had. "I think you might be right," she replied.

Aisling turned away from the Maytree and started wandering among the graves. She scanned the headstones as she walked. Some were so faded and weatherworn, or covered with lichen that she couldn't read them. Those had to be several centuries old, more than a hundred years. She found one grave dating from around the time of the Titanic and noted the style and location, then looked for more of a similar type. The engraved names and dates could be easily read. Aisling searched every one until she was sure she hadn't missed a single one.

"Are you looking for Jimbo's grave?" said Liv, behind her.

"Yes, and I'm not finding it. That can only mean a couple of things." Aisling wet her lips. "Either he doesn't have a gravestone, which would be strange considering all the other ones from the turn of last century and around the time of the Titanic have headstones. Or it could be that–"

Liv cut her off. "That he isn't buried here?"

"No, he told me that he was in here somewhere, he was sure of it. But it could be that the Sidhe took his body into their realm. But why would they do that? What would they want with Jimbo?"

Liv shrugged. "He must be special to them, for some reason. Either that, or he did something bad to them and they wanted to take revenge on him."

Aisling sighed. "I haven't seen him in a week since Yuletide. He doesn't want me to contact him again in case I put myself in danger, but I have no choice. I'm going to have force contact with him again. He's the only one who can give me answers about what's going on."

Chapter twelve

Aisling's bright phone screen dazzled her eyes as she sat in her dim living room while snowflakes danced outside. Liv had given her what she needed to know about hawthorn; now Aisling scanned the screen, educating herself about holly.

"For over a thousand years, people brought holly into their homes to protect themselves from malevolent fairies. Holly also allows fairies to shelter inside homes without causing friction between them and the human occupants," Aisling read aloud.

Liv jumped out of her chair as though she'd been stung and hurried out of the house. Aisling watched her through the living room window as she snatched a sprig of holly from the bush in the garden and hurried back inside.

Aisling threw her head back laughing. "You're even more afraid of the Sidhe than I am."

"I'm not taking any chances," said Liv, her head cocked to one side. "If you're going to contact Jimbo, you want to make sure you don't invite any harmful entities into your house."

Having such a cautious friend was proving to be most useful, especially for what Aisling planned to do next. But first she needed to learn more. Aisling continued. "Holly trees also give protection from lightning, which is why they're traditionally planted near houses. The spines on their leaves act as miniature lightning conductors and this protects both the holly tree and other nearby objects."

Aisling thought of what she had discussed with Eoin the previous day. The plan to use the Newton's Cradle in conjunction with the fairy lights and her golf umbrella to contact Jimbo involved channelling electricity. It wasn't the same thing as lightning, but it was similar enough; if holly was a lightning conductor, would this help channel all the electricity into her body?

"I have a plan. I'm going to get everything set up. Can you message Eoin and get him to come over, if he's free? We talked the other day and he said he wants to be in on this," said Aisling.

"In on what? The plan to contact Jimbo?"

Aisling grabbed the sprig of holly that Liv had brought inside and added it to her string necklace along with the one she already had. "No. The plan to get my spirit over into the Netherworld, the Sidhe Realm, not to bring Jimbo's here. I'm going to use the Newton's Cradle and the fairy lights to make an electrical channel that I can harness with the umbrella over there."

Liv gawked. "You're planning to do – what?"

"Just text him." Aisling pointed at Liv's phone, urging her to hurry.

Aisling grabbed the Newton's Cradle and golf umbrella and hurried upstairs to switch on the fairy lights. She stopped halfway up at the sound of Liv on the phone and Eoin's muffled voice on the other end.

"I tried to tell her it's a bad idea. It could be dangerous," said Eoin.

"I didn't know she was planning to electrocute herself. Can you come over and talk some sense into her?"

"I'll try, but she's pretty set on it. I'm surprised she didn't do it sooner, in fact. We talked about it yesterday. I was worried that she might have tried it after I left. I'm glad she didn't do anything stupid while she was alone."

"We can't let her fry herself. Get over here fast, please."

Silence. Aisling gritted her teeth. "I'm not going to fry myself. It's not like I'm going to stick a fork into a socket, or anything," she shouted downstairs.

Liv came out of the living room and climbed the stairs to where Aisling stood, halfway up. "This is a bad idea, Aisling. If you need to contact Jimbo, why can't you hire a professional? We could get in contact with a medium and do a proper séance instead," said Liv, an edge of desperation in her voice.

"You both talked about me there like I was a kid who doesn't know any better. But I'm the one who has been in contact with Jimbo – and he wouldn't be warning me to break contact unless I was on the right track," Aisling spat.

"That's exactly what Eoin and I are saying – of course you're on the right track. You'll end up killing yourself and going over into the Sidhe Realm for real, but you'll be dead too." Liv's voice was pleading. "Don't do this – let me find a medium."

Aisling shook her head. "I'm going to do this whether you're here, or not. But I'd rather you were here just in case there are any complications."

"Like you dying, you mean. I can't stand by here and let you voluntarily kill yourself. I think this is reckless." Liv's voice had a definite note of panic. She stood in the hallway, glancing at the door, then back to Aisling and again to the door.

"I'll wait for Eoin before I do it. But neither of you can stop me. I need to try this," said Aisling. She knew she sounded stubborn, and was being completely selfish by disregarding her friends' warnings, but she was in too far now. Jimbo wanted her to stay away too for her own safety; but his spirit was trapped in the Sidhe Realm and couldn't get to heaven. It was up to her to set him free.

Liv hurried to the front door and let Eoin in. He bent double, panting, then straightened himself and leaned against the wall to catch his breath.

"She won't listen, she's going to do it," said Liv.

"I found out that Jimbo is trapped in the Netherworld," said Aisling, ignoring Liv. "He's in the Sidhe Realm. They took his body from Friar's Bush Graveyard on the first of May. They might even have killed him, for all I know. I have to set his spirit free so he can leave the Netherworld and go towards the light."

Liv threw up her hands in a defeated gesture as she looked at Eoin. Eoin was pale, his face alarmed.

"You told me you were going to find a way to do this experiment safely," he said. "You promised."

"And I will," Aisling sighed, exasperated. "This holly will protect me. Tell him, Liv. Tell him what we found out about holly – the research we did."

"People use it for protection against malevolent fairies. It's also useful to keep things safe against lightning."

Aisling smiled to herself, satisfied that Liv had gotten the facts mixed up, as she had been counting on. Liv thought that holly would deflect electricity away; instead, it would act as a conductor and channel the energy directly through Aisling, since she wore it as a necklace.

"See?" Aisling showed the holly on a string around her neck. "I've got my guarantee of success right here."

She could tell her friends were reluctant witnesses, but had resigned themselves to the fact that she was going through with it no matter what. Liv and Eoin exchanged furtive glances, then followed Aisling upstairs.

Aisling set the Newton's Cradle in motion on the landing and placed the metal shaft of the umbrella on top of the frame. She switched on the fairy lights and touched the metal ferrule at the tip against the USB port at the base of the plug. The reaction was instantaneous. Cold pain seized her body, starting from her left hand where she touched the umbrella to the fairy lights and spreading across to her right hand where the umbrella touched the Newton's Cradle. In the split second that she was able to think, Aisling likened it to the sensation of pain from a nerve being drilled in her tooth at the dentist. Neon snakes sizzled before her eyes and everything in front of her became white. The pain had gone; now she felt nothing. Her body must surely be numb?

The brightness subsided. Her house reappeared around her, everything in its familiar place except Liv and Eoin. They were gone. Aisling looked around. On second glance, her house was different; changed. There was a darkness surrounding everything, as though mist engulfed all her possessions. Could she be in the Netherworld?

"Jimbo? Are you here?"

No answer. Aisling walked downstairs and stepped out her front door. The street outside was also dark and shadowy, as though she were wearing sunglasses. She turned and looked back at her house. It looked faded like a photo negative impression of her house and not the real place. Creepy.

Aisling walked down the street instead of going uphill towards Stranmillis Road. She turned left and walked towards Botanic Gardens. Everything around her swam in darkness, shadows more pronounced and movement in dark corners. She trained her eyes on a tree, trying to discern the source of the movement and saw a wavering shadowy figure, just as Jimbo had appeared to her in her house in the real world.

"Jimbo? Is that you?"

No response. The shadow figure skulked and she heard the dry, crisp noise of rustling leaves as it moved out of sight.

Where was this place? Was this really the Sidhe Realm? Aisling hadn't given it much thought, but she would have imagined the place where fairies resided to be full of brightness and majesty; an eternal spring time with nature in full bloom. Not a dismal place that suggested death – or worse.

Aisling looped through photo negative Botanic Gardens and turned left again up Stranmillis Road. It was deserted; devoid of both people and cars. If ever there would be a post-apocalyptic Belfast, this would be it.

When she got to Friar's Bush Graveyard, Aisling stopped and made one more left turn. The sound of singing met her ears; a female voice, high-pitched and sweet sounding, but not a woman. As she approached the source of the singing, Aisling saw Cliona crouched beneath the Maytree. Cliona glowed moon bright, a beacon of light in the dark shadows.

"Aisling. You came back. Closer this time, I see," said Cliona.

"Where's Jimbo?"

"You won't find him here. You're closer, but not close enough. Did you drink the tea I made?"

Aisling remembered Jimbo's advice; she reached for the holly necklace, ready to brandish it at Cliona. But the berries were shrivelled and the spiky leaves curled and black. The electricity must have charred it when it got channelled through them both.

"Oh, what a shame your amulet of protection is damaged," said Cliona, her voice full of sarcasm.

Aisling looked at what Cliona was doing and saw a ring of mushrooms planted in the grass surrounding the Maytree. Cliona touched the grass with forefinger and another appeared, then another, until a perfect *Fairy Ring* encircled it.

"Am I in the Sidhe Realm? Is this the Netherworld where Jimbo is stuck?"

A devious smile spread across Cliona's face. "Sadly for you, no. But you're getting closer. Try harder next time."

Aisling's forehead tensed. "If this isn't where the Sidhe live, then where am I?"

"You could call it a limbo world between your world and that of the Sidhe. You managed to shock yourself, but you're not dead and neither are you quite alive," Cliona chortled.

"So you're saying, this is an out of body experience, or something? I got here because I knocked myself unconscious with an electrical shock?"

"Mm-hmm," said Cliona. "Eat one of these. It'll help you get back to your world."

Aisling looked at the mushroom in Cliona's hand. Was it a magic mushroom? A poisonous toadstool, perhaps?

"I'm done with taking food or drinks from you." Aisling backed off a few steps, not taking her eyes off Cliona.

She was about to leave when she noticed that the turf below her feet felt spongy and wet. Water pooled around the roots of hawthorn tree. Where was it coming from? Aisling's eyes followed the trickling water as it pooled in areas where the grass was sparse. Further to the right, the water ran as tiny streams. She followed it for about ten feet, weaving between the headstones, and noticed a small, narrow stream, about a foot wide. There was no stream in the real world in such a location. Was it a spiritual tributary of the River Lagan, following an ancient course, maybe? Aisling followed it, pushing through bushes and branches; there weren't the same boundaries of walls and the back yards of houses beyond Friar's Bush Graveyard as there were in the real world. Except for one. She stopped walking, her feet on either side of the stream. It led directly to her front garden, where it passed under the holly bush and became a swamp of leaves and mud touching the wall below the bay window of her living room. Aisling was sure the stream continued to flow under her house and past it on the other side. But to where?

Chapter thirteen

"Oh my gosh, Aisling. Aisling!"

Aisling felt the sting of a hand on her face, slapping her right cheek. She blinked her eyes open and looked around, then raised her head up to get her bearings. She was sprawled on her stairs with Liv crouching on the step above her head and Eoin on the bottom step, his face wild with fear.

"I'm back," she said, weak through her parched throat. "I made it back."

Liv and Eoin helped her up and took her into the living room.

"Please don't ever do that again. I'm only willing to see that happen once in my lifetime," said Eoin, his voice strained.

"You got fried. See? I told you that would happen," said Liv.

Eoin nudged her with his elbow. "It's not the time for guilt trips. She's barely alive."

"I saw Cliona. But not Jimbo. I didn't make it into the Sidhe Realm. I was in a limbo place between the real world and the Sidhe world. Jimbo was right. He told me there are many worlds."

"Heaven and hell is enough for me." Liv let go of Aisling's underarm and walked into the kitchen. She returned with a glass of water and handed it to her. Aisling gulped it all down in one.

"You were knocked out. There was a bright flash of white and a zapping noise. You lit up like a flippin' Christmas tree," said Eoin, his eyes wide behind his glasses.

"You scared the shit out of us both. We thought you were dead," Liv added.

Aisling ignored both of them. She needed to remember all the details of the limbo place before they faded from her mind. "Eoin, could you grab a sheet out of my printer there? It's on the top shelf."

Eoin handed her the paper and Aisling sat at the table by the window. She grabbed a pencil from her pencil case and drew a square with a triangle on top for her house in the middle of the sheet. Next, she drew a large splodge in the bottom left and labelled it Botanic Gardens, then a medium sized splodge, which she labelled Friar's Bush. A wiggly line from Friar's Bush to her house showed the stream she had seen in the limbo world. Last, she added a few spirals at the start of the stream in Friar's Bush and wrote hawthorn tree then added more spirals in front of her house where the stream ended and wrote that this was the holly bush. Aisling looked at the crude map she had drawn. It wasn't quite right. She put pencil to paper again and extended the wiggly lines for the stream so that it continued down to the bottom of the page and upwards to the top. What else did the stream in the limbo world connect in the real world?

Aisling looked at her friends' puzzled faces; an explanation was in order. Liv and Eoin listened as she told them of her journey, Liv looking disturbed and Eoin fearful. She made sure to describe the shadow figure she had seen hiding behind a tree in Botanic Gardens and Cliona planting a fairy ring of mushrooms in Friar's Bush.

"It's all very strange and interesting," Liv said, with a furtive glance at Eoin before continuing. "But I'd rather you contacted a medium than electrocute yourself again."

"It clearly works though, doesn't it?" Aisling shrugged to brush off their worries. "I know I didn't see Jimbo, like another time when I accidentally got an electric shock off the kettle and was able to talk to him up in the attic–"

"You what? You never told me that you were electrocuted once already?" said Eoin, his mouth agape.

"Me neither," said Liv, her cheeks red.

"It was by accident. I was a bit tipsy, and maybe a bit careless too. I was upset after class on that Monday after my party." She glanced at Liv, who blushed an even deeper shade of crimson. "This time of year is hard for me. My mum died on Christmas Eve when I was eight years old."

Silence fell as Liv and Eoin digested her words.

"Aisling, I'm so sorry." Liv grabbed her hands and rubbed them with her thumbs. Liv's hands were soft and warm around her own.

"That's rough," said Eoin, shaking his head. "What happened, if you don't mind saying?"

Aisling gave a tight-lipped smile. "It's alright. I'm able to talk about it now without crying. We were over at my uncle's house for our usual big family gathering. My mum was putting the lights on his Christmas tree. I don't really remember what happened next – she just seemed to have a sudden seizure and didn't come back round after that. I was so afraid, all I recall is screaming and screaming. We moved our family get-together to Boxing Day after that and Uncle Gerry always remembers to take down the Christmas tree before we all arrive."

"Oh honey, that's awful," Liv cried.

"Did your mum have epilepsy?" said Eoin.

"She must have had it since a seizure is what killed her, although none of us had ever known her to have one before. Dad insisted she had epilepsy to sooth Naoise and I at times when we couldn't stop ourselves crying in the first few years after her death. It brought the three of us together – Naoise, dad and I – but it also drove us apart too. Even now when we meet up back home, there'll be times when all three of us just sit in silence, not even looking at each other. It's not quite a hostile silence, but it's awkward. It's like there's so much we want to say, but we also don't want to cause any more hurt, if you get what I mean?"

"I'm surprised you're even able to have a Christmas tree in your house after that," said Liv.

Aisling glanced at the tree. "I suppose in a weird way, it comforts me. I sometimes stare into a single bauble, up so close my nose almost touches it, and imagine that she's standing behind me with her hand on my shoulder. I like to imagine I can see her smiling at me, her face full of love."

Liv and Eoin looked haunted as they stared at her.

Aisling wiped a tear away and sniffed. "But enough of all that. I've finally come round to your plan, Liv. It seems that I'm not able to get into the Sidhe Realm by myself, as I ended up in that limbo world, and I don't seem to have any control about when or how I can reach Jimbo either. Jimbo doesn't even want me to contact him out of fear that I might injure myself and he's right. So I think the best plan now is for me to find a medium who can help guide me into the Sidhe Realm, the Netherworld as Jimbo calls it, in a safer way than electrocuting myself."

Eoin looked dubious. "I don't think that's what mediums do though, Aisling. They're spirit guides, they bring the dead to the living, not the living to the dead."

Liv's eyes were glazed at she stared at Aisling, deep in thought. "A medium could draw Jimbo to you though, which would force him to give you answers. You could think up a list of things you want to ask him and I could search for a medium who seems good."

Aisling looked out into the stairwell at the fairy lights for inspiration. What did she want to ask Jimbo? She flipped her map over and started writing questions on the blank page.

"Do you realise you aren't buried in Friar's Bush and that the fairies took your dead body into the Sidhe Realm?" Aisling recited as she wrote.

"How about, 'Do you know why you're so important to the Sidhe?' as he might not even know," said Eoin.

"What do you know about Cliona?" Aisling wrote each word as she spoke it.

"Do you know there's a stream running from Friar's Bush Graveyard to this house," said Eoin.

"Our house," Aisling corrected and jotted down the question.

"Why is electricity so important to contact you?" Eoin suggested.

"That one's obvious. It's because it's energy that connects the different worlds," Aisling answered. She wracked her brain to try and think of more questions.

"I know," said Liv. "How can we get you out of the Fairy Realm so you can go towards the light?"

"Oh, that's a good one," said Aisling. She wrote it down, but her excitement quickly dissipated into sadness. "I guess I'll be sad though if Jimbo goes to heaven. I've kind of become attached to him."

Liv guffawed. "Don't tell me you're in love with a ghost?"

"Are you?" Eoin's forehead crumpled.

Aisling rolled her eyes at her friends. "Not love exactly, I hardly know him. He's become like a good friend over these past couple of weeks."

Liv clapped her hands and stamped her feet, rolling her head back as she laughed. "Brilliant! You *do* love him. Oh, you are the *nerdiest* person I know."

"That's so wrong," Eoin huffed. "There's loads of men in the real world, you don't need one who's dead."

Aisling laughed with Liv. Eoin's grumpy expression dissolved and he managed a smile. Liv turned her attention back to her phone and Aisling watched over her shoulder as she searched for 'mediums in Belfast' before scrolling down the list of suggested businesses. Her finger hovered over one with 50 ratings of above

4.5 stars under the title 'Craig psychic medium'. "Here, I've found a medium that sounds promising. I'm going to try to give him a ring. You'll be in touch with your lover-boy soon."

Chapter fourteen

L iv and Eoin helped to clear the table of all Aisling's lecture notes, textbooks and stationery to make room for Craig the psychic medium, to fill the space with spiritual objects conducive to communicating with the other world. Craig's rainbow coloured tie-dye slacks swished as he bustled about the table. Together with his shoulder-length mousey hair and linen tunic top, he looked like he had come straight off a plane from Bali, rather than someone accustomed to midwinter in Belfast. He was older than Aisling had imagined too, looking to be in his mid-forties, not twenties as she had guessed by his profession.

Aisling dumped her course materials on the window ledge and set a sprig of fresh holly, taken from the bush in her garden, on top of them and a bottle of water, with a dash of Pixie Pear tea, the last drop strained from the berries and leaves Cliona had given her at Yuletide. Hawthorn would help her spirit to journey into the Sidhe Realm. Holly would help repel the Sidhe while she was there, so that she could hopefully locate Jimbo.

"Before we begin, I would ask that you turn off your mobile phones and any other objects that cause electrical interference – tablets, laptops and so on," Craig began.

All three switched off their phones. Aisling checked that her laptop on the sofa was switched off too.

"Here is a white candle to call the spirits forth with its light and warmth." Craig placed the white church candle in the middle of the table and lit it.

"Here are three amethyst crystals, placed to the East, their purple beauty to attract psychic energy into this home," Craig said.

Aisling watched him set them to the right side of the white candle, spaced a foot away. She recalled a poem from her youth helping her to chart the direction: *Never Eat Soggy Wheat.* Or something like that. It worked in any event; she noted that Craig had indeed set the amethysts to the east side.

"Find here salt, positioned West, which will cleanse and purify the energy coming into this house, and ward off bad spirits," Craig continued. He set a small earthen bowl on the table to the left side of the white candle.

"Now find the Pendulum of Knowledge, delivered North. May it guide the spirits to give us appropriate answers," he said.

Craig arranged what looked like a small, golden retort stand on the table and fastened a crystal, suspended on a gold chain, to the clamp so that it dangled an inch above the wood. It sat above the candle in the middle.

"Find now the last and most important object, the Tree of Life book, lovingly placed to the South." Craig set a small pocketbook, covered in tan-coloured leather, towards the bottom of the table. It had an engraved emblem of a tree inside a circle on the front. "May it instil in us the right questions to find what we seek."

Craig turned to Aisling, Liv and Eoin with a placid smile, his hands held wide in an open gesture. "I now invite you to sit around the table. Aisling facing North, Eoin facing East, Liv facing West and myself facing South."

Aisling took her seat facing the bay window of her living room. Should she ask the significance of where they sat? Craig didn't say. Maybe it wasn't important. Best not to interrupt the medium's flow, though.

"Take the hand of the person on either side of you. Try to stay connected at all times through the process, as it will help create a stronger connection for the spirits." Craig closed his eyes. He inhaled through his nose, his chest rising and exhaled through an open mouth. Aisling, facing him, felt her fringe blow as the air expelled over her.

"We are here tonight to contact the man who in life was called Jim Murphy and otherwise known as Jimbo."

Aisling was impressed. Craig had certainly done his homework, memorising the information she had messaged across to him.

"If you are there, please make your presence known."

Barely a second had passed when the crystal moved a fraction of an inch, as though an invisible finger had pushed it. Liv gasped and Craig directed a calming smile towards her.

"I am going to invite you now, Jimbo, to enter my physical body so that you may communicate with Aisling. She wishes to talk to you. If you understand my request, please indicate to us that you are happy to proceed," said Craig.

The crystal jiggled again. Eoin peered at it over the rim of his glasses, his eyes wide. Liv's neck was hollowed out as though she were holding her breath. Aisling turned her attention back to the crystal and then across to Craig in turn.

Craig's calm demeanour changed; his rounded shoulders became angular, and his curved back grew straight. His benign smile dropped, and a serious expression set on his face.

"Aisling," said Craig.

His eyes were glazed, a mistiness over his irises, as though he were hypnotised. Aisling understood; Jimbo was speaking now, not Craig.

"Jimbo? Are you mad at me for calling you here?"

Jimbo shook his head. "I could never be mad at you. A little frustrated, perhaps, as you went against my wishes, but I appreciate your care."

Liv shot Aisling a teasing smile, that Aisling couldn't help returning. She knew Liv wanted to make a joke about how she was in love with a ghost, but didn't want to interrupt the séance. She pulled the sheet of paper with her questions out of her pocket; who knew how long Jimbo could stay?

"Do you realise you aren't buried in Friar's Bush and that the fairies took your dead body into the Sidhe Realm?"

"I didn't know that," said Jimbo, his voice sad. "But I'm not surprised either. They have very mysterious ways."

"Do you know why you might be so important to the Sidhe?" she said.

Jimbo pursed his lips. "I can't say for sure. I keep away from them in the Netherworld, and stay unnoticed as much as I can. I think I must have angered them. I pried into their business too much, and offended them by planting the holly bush out in the garden. Holly repels them."

Aisling glanced at the next question on her list. "What do you know about Cliona?"

"She isn't one of them – she's not Sidhe. But she isn't human either. I think she could be a deity."

"A deity? You mean, like a goddess?"

"I don't know. I can't find out much in my current existence. I'm alone in there. I have no friends, but I have many enemies," said Jimbo.

"What do you know about the stream running from Friar's Bush Graveyard to this house?" said Aisling.

Jimbo – Craig – looked troubled. "There's a stream right in this location in the Netherworld. There are many places of water in that realm. I don't know the significance."

So much for Craig's Pendulum of Knowledge; poor Jimbo didn't seem to know any more than she did. Less, in fact. The questions were getting her nowhere. Aisling skipped over the electricity one to the last question and gulped. This was the one she wanted to ask least of all. But for Jimbo's sake, she had to do it.

"How can we get you out of the Sidhe Realm so you can go towards the light?"

Jimbo shook his head. "There is no way out of the Netherworld. There is no light."

"There must be a way out – you must be able to move on somehow. There is always a way out of purgatory into heaven. If souls can get out of purgatory, then you can get out of the Sidhe Realm as well." Aisling willed him to think – of something, anything. It couldn't be impossible; could it? The thought of Jimbo stuck in a realm where he wasn't supposed to be, away from his loved ones, was depressing.

Craig's body jolted in his seat. His eyes bulged and he coughed, gasping for breath. Jimbo was gone.

"Well, that got us nowhere," Eoin moaned.

"Did Jimbo make contact? I feel the residue of the spiritual world all around us. It prickles my very skin," said Craig. "What happened when I went into my receptive state?"

"He took over your body as you asked," said Aisling.

Craig looked eager. "What about the questions you had for him?"

She pursed her lips. "He didn't know any more than we do. They're keeping a lot hidden from him. He's trapped – he can't even move towards the light."

"I have one more thing I can try. Hopefully it will help him move on from the place of fairies. I'm going to have to go into a trance again, though this time my body will not become a conduit for Jimbo's soul." Craig let go of Liv and Eoin's hands. With a sting of surprise, Aisling saw that he produced the Newton's

Cradle and set it in the centre of the table, removing the white candle instead.

"Normally I would ask that any electrical objects that interfere with energy are removed before a séance – this is why I needed you to switch off your phones. However, I considered your questions with care, including the one you had answered yourself – why is electricity so important to contact Jimbo?" Craig took a deep breath, before continuing. "In order for me to help a spirit move on, I need to reach a state of hypnosis. The Newton's Cradle will be sufficient to help me reach a trance-like state and all the while should serve to attract Jimbo's aura. I am going to use it to guide him towards the light."

Craig set the Newton's Cradle in motion, lifting three balls on one side, causing three balls to lift on the opposite side. Aisling reminded herself of the Law of Conservation of Energy: *Energy can be neither created nor destroyed, it can only be converted from one form into another.*

Could Jimbo be converted from spirit form in the Sidhe Realm to spirit form in heaven?

Craig's eyes were glazed again, but this time there was a sleepy heaviness to them rather than the mist that had clouded them when Jimbo had taken over his body.

"Jimbo. Jim Murphy. Are you still there? If you are, give us a sign of your presence," said Craig.

The crystal hanging on the Pendulum of Knowledge moved a fraction.

"I am going to help you now." Craig picked up the white candle. It was still lit, though the wax had burned lower by an inch. "Can you see my flame? Let me know if you can?"

The crystal moved again.

"Good. Walk towards my flame. It will guide you into the light."

Aisling heard a morose voice in her mind. *There is no light, apart from the candle flame.* "He says he can't see any light, there is no light."

"He will see it soon," said Craig, his voice full of confident authority. "Jimbo, I need you to be strong and believe. Follow my candle flame. Are you doing that?"

"He is," said Aisling. "He wants to go into the light as much as we want him to, but there is no light."

"You're almost there, Jimbo. Picture the light. It's a pinprick on the dark horizon at first, but it's growing bigger. See it now as a white circle the size of your thumbnail, if you hold up your hand. Now look. It's as big as your hand and it's spreading. Soon it will be all around you. Do you see it, Jim Murphy, do you see it?"

Aisling gritted her teeth hard, trying to concentrate her energy on the channel in her mind. "I can't hear him anymore. I think he's gone. I think you must have sent him on."

Craig's eyes refocused and he looked at her. "No. He didn't make it into the light, he was right. There was no light. It doesn't make any sense – the light always appears for spirits when it is called, the tunnel towards heaven never fails. Something is really wrong here. Jimbo is really stuck. We need to try another plan to rescue him."

Chapter fifteen

"Follow my voice. My voice will guide you in the darkness."

Craig's voice was disembodied in the gloom. The clicking of the Newton's Cradle had faded; now all Aisling heard were his words, lingering in the darkness.

"Don't be afraid. My voice is with you on your journey. It will be a source of comfort as you enter the Sidhe Realm," said Craig.

Aisling moved her feet, but it was like walking through thick mud. She couldn't tell if she was moving at all. Her legs were heavy and she had no sense of direction. Unlike the last time after she had received an electric shock, and had been stuck between the real world and Sidhe Realm, this place was entirely black. It was a place of nothing, anti-existence.

"Your body is asleep, so you are unable to talk or move in the real world," Craig's voice called. "Your spirit moves freely in the beyond. If you have reached the Sidhe Realm, can you please use your mind to let us know? Swing the Pendulum of Knowledge and I will understand you. Left for yes, right for no."

Aisling willed her mind: right for no.

"Aisling, I await your communication," Craig's gentle voice appealed.

Right for no, swing right for no.

"You should be entering the Sidhe Realm soon. You should see a bright flash of light as your spirit passes across into the plane of existence that Jimbo knows as the Netherworld," said Craig.

Why wasn't it working? Why was she unable to move the Pendulum of Knowledge with her mind?

"I am going to have to ask you to return to us, Aisling, if you are unable to communicate soon," said Craig.

"No," said another voice; high-pitched and feminine. "Don't listen to him."

Aisling gasped. "Who are you? Where are you? Show yourself."

"Aisling, I now ask you to return. Follow my voice," Craig continued.

"I'm so glad you can hear me," said the female voice. "Come to me instead, don't leave."

Aisling spun in circles, trying to see, but all was black. "Cliona? If that's you, stay away."

"Aisling," Craig's voice echoed, "I shine the light of the white candle now, so that you may follow its flame. Come towards it."

She turned wildly around until she was light-headed. There was no candle flame, in any direction.

"Honey, don't go," said the woman's voice.

Honey? Aisling tried to squint, but her eyes couldn't discern anything. The feminine voice was familiar. Where did she know it from? She was sure she had heard it before.

A warm, gentle pressure appeared on her left wrist. Aisling reached for it and felt a soft but firm hand on her arm. "Let go of me. Who are you?"

"Don't be afraid. You're lost. I'm going to take you to a safe place where we can talk."

The more the woman spoke, the more familiar her voice seemed. Aisling forced her brain to think, but she came up with nothing.

Gradually the blackness began to change. Dark grey cloud enveloped her. Aisling was able to see the silhouette of a woman in front of her, leading her by the wrist. The woman had black, shoulder-length hair and a slight build. She was maybe shorter than Aisling by an inch or so. If Aisling were being rational, she would have shaken herself free of the woman's grasp; but her heart guided her, not her head. She let her arm remain limp in the woman's grip and didn't pull back.

It took a moment for Aisling to realise she could no longer hear Craig's voice. She had to trust in the kindness of the stranger who led her, for all she knew, further into the depths of whatever limbo existence she was stuck in.

The dark grey clouds faded further and Aisling could see that she was in a place of swirling silver-grey fog. White silhouettes of trees came into focus, like reverse negatives. What was this strange place?

The woman leading Aisling slowly turned and as her face came into view, a strangled scream forced its way out of her throat and was lost in the still air.

"Aisling, honey. How long has it been? A decade?"

Her mum's smiling face dissolved in a pool of tears as Aisling's eyes swam. She let her body succumb to sobs and felt her mum's arms around her, pulling her head down onto her shoulder.

"Eleven years," Aisling hiccoughed. "I'm nineteen now."

"You don't know how long I've waited to see you. I've longed to hold you again," said her mum.

Aisling sniffed and wiped tears on the back of her hand. "I don't remember you being so small, mum."

"I was big to an eight year old, honey." Her mum stroked her hair, soothing her.

"Why are you here? Don't tell me you were taken into the Sidhe Realm too? I thought you were in heaven," Aisling said, before a fresh wave of sobs overtook her.

"This isn't the Sidhe Realm. You haven't managed to cross over. As much as I want to talk to you, I need you to listen to me and stop this. It's dangerous."

"I'm not afraid of death." Aisling's body shook uncontrollably. "How could I be when I know you're here looking out for me?"

Her mum lowered her eyes and Aisling saw that they were sad. "It isn't your time to go yet, darling. If you were to accidentally pass over, in this fruitless attempt to contact Jim Murphy, it would be before your time. This pursuit is reckless."

"But don't you see? Now that I have proof that there are many worlds, beyond the real one, how could I not want to explore? What would death be, other than a few moments of pain?" said Aisling.

Pain. Her mum looked pained. More in pain than she had ever seen her before.

Or not. Aisling's chest tightened as a memory flooded back.

Aisling was sitting on Uncle Gerry's shaggy, brown living room rug. She poked the tip of her forefinger through the string loop of a golden bauble and watched it spin as it dangled. Mum was behind her, threading the fairy lights through the branches of the pine tree; Aisling could see her reflection in the golden bauble.

She forced her mind back to the present, cutting the memory short, and realised she had been wincing.

"Don't do this. You're not ready to deal with the painful truth," said her mum.

She sniffed tears away. "It was a happy memory, not a painful truth. I want it to stay a happy memory. I want to hold on to the thought of you, as you were then, alive."

Her mum took Aisling's hand within both of her own and rubbed it. "The reason you've come to this place and not the Sidhe Realm, or the shadowy limbo existence you went to after the electric shock is that you need to deal with some truths first – you've been taken here until you can face your past – but I don't know if you are ready."

"No, I came here because Craig guided me here by accident. But it's been a blessing in disguise because I've found you," said Aisling.

"This is a place where souls go after they die – the Spirit World – where they wait to transcend. You're being blocked from moving into either the Sidhe Realm, or going back to the real world." Her mum was emphatic, making Aisling stop sniffing, or sobbing, and stare at her.

"Are you saying that I'm dead, for real? That can't be right."

"No, you're still alive, but barely. You're in spirit form. I should know – my spirit has been here for the past eleven years in earth years – real world time. I can move easily through the different planes of existence. The ones on a lower vibration, like the real world, the Sidhe Realm and the Plane of Light."

"Plane of Light? Is that what you call this place?" said Aisling.

Her mum nodded, a peaceable smile on her face. "It's a nicer term than the Spirit World, which frightens me, somehow. People enter the Plane of Light when they're dead. Or, as you have done, through their deep unconscious mind. Your body on earth is in a coma state at the moment, which is why you've come here."

"So you're saying, the Plane of Light isn't heaven? For me, it's nothing more than a dying part of my unconscious brain?" said Aisling, her voice cracking.

Her mum sighed, long and slow. "Honey, I worry you're too young to process all of this. It's too much for you. I want you to go back to the real world and don't try to tamper anymore with things that are dead. Dead, and better off dead."

Aisling pulled her hand out of her mum's grasp. "No, you're wrong. You're dead and Jimbo is dead and neither of you are at peace. How can you ask me not to help? I can't let either of you stay trapped – Jimbo in the shadowy Sidhe Realm and you floating between the lower planes of existence, unable to move on to planes of 'higher vibration' – I'm assuming by that, you mean heaven?"

Mum nodded. "Yes, darling. Heaven is the plane of the highest vibration, where souls go once they transcend."

"Well, it's up to me to help you get there." Aisling sounded defiant; she couldn't keep it out of her voice. "I have to save you."

She pressed her eyes shut and focused on the memory of her mum's reflection, shining and happy in the golden bauble as she hung the fairy lights on the Christmas tree at Uncle Gerry's house. A happy memory. Aisling clenched her teeth, etching the memory in her mind to preserve it as it was; not a moment before, or a moment after.

"You're trying too hard. This isn't how you go about saving me," said her mum.

Aisling pressed her thumbs into the corners of her eyes, forcing tears back. She held onto the memory, as best she could.

"It wasn't your fault," mum said, barely a whisper.

"I know, you had a seizure. You died of epilepsy. Dad said so," said Aisling.

She heard her mum's weary sigh, though she still didn't open her eyes. "I didn't have a seizure. I didn't have epilepsy. Your dad told you that to protect you. To shield you from the truth."

Aisling's eyes snapped open. But instead of seeing her mum and the photo-negative trees, she saw the rest of the memory play out in her mind, like a cinema reel.

Her mum had finished stringing the fairy lights around the tree. She stayed on the metal stepladder and pointed to the plug, on the floor. Aisling grabbed the plug and reached towards the socket.

"Stop it. Why are you showing me this?" Aisling cried.

"I'm not. Your subconscious is showing it to you. You blocked it out for eleven years, but now you need to face it."

Aisling reached to put it in the socket, but the plug slipped from her hand. It dropped and fell with a splash into the bucket of water which held the tree trunk.

"I can't, mum, I can't see this."

"You already did. Once."

Aisling wiped the plug on her Christmas jumper. Mum didn't pay any heed; she was busy fluffing out the branches, ready to put the baubles on next. She climbed down and took the plug from Aisling, then pushed it into the socket and switched it on.

A white flash. A horrible, sizzling, burning smell. Smoke. So much smoke. And screams. So many screams. Her own screams; the screams of a child in terror, an innocent girl forced to grow up too soon.

A choking, rasping cry spluttered its way out of Aisling's chest. She clapped both hands over her face, but couldn't stifle it.

"Mum, I'm so sorry. It was me, all along, it was my fault. I did it. I'm the reason you died."

Aisling crumpled onto her mum's lap and let herself be cradled. Mum shushed her and soothed her. Was she deserving of such comfort? She couldn't say; but she couldn't do anything other than cry. Dissolve into tears; a dozen years of pent-up guilt, denial, memory blackouts and now?

"I didn't know it was dangerous, mum. I didn't know that water and electricity could kill a person. I didn't know."

"Ssh, it's alright. You buried it for eleven years, but you finally faced it. You should be proud."

"I'm not proud of causing your death by my own stupidity and carelessness," Aisling sobbed.

"You were a child. It's in the past. I'm free of pain. And now you are too. You're free to move past this hurt and find your own path."

Aisling raised her head from her mum's lap and looked at her, through wet eyelashes. "Then I know what my path is. It's to save people from now on, not cause them harm. I'm going to start with Jimbo. I have to help him, mum. It's my destiny."

Chapter sixteen

Cold sweat coated every part of Aisling as her body reawakened in the real world with a jolt. Her limbs felt numb at first, then gradually her fingers and toes became tingly and feeling started to return all over. Craig hovered over her, holding the Tree of Life book, and Aisling fixated on its wide branches and spreading roots encapsulated within a circle, imagining it instilling its life energy into her body and mind.

She was still sitting in her chair at the table; at least she hadn't ended up on the floor, having a fit. Thinking of seizures brought her mind back to her mum. Tears began to form in the corners of her eyes and she shut them, letting her eyelids become dams, suppressing all the feelings she had about the place she had just been, mere moments before.

"We thought we had lost you. We thought you were dead," Liv cried.

"Where did you go? Could you not see the White Candle flame?" Craig's eyes were wide with concern.

Aisling looked at the White Candle, its flame burning low and only two inches of the wax left. How long had they been doing the séance? "I could hear you trying to call me back – at first. But then your voice disappeared," she said.

Craig was relieved. "I'm glad to know there was a connection in the first place. What disrupted it? Were you accosted by angry spirits?"

"Not angry ones, no. I met my mum," she said.

Craig, Liv and Eoin watched her in momentary silence. Aisling was happy for the pause in conversation, allowing her to recall all that had happened.

The medium's face broke into a delighted smile. "This is a good omen, a better one than I could have hoped for. There is no better spirit guide for a person than a blood relative. Can you tell us what happened?"

What indeed. So much had taken place. Aisling swallowed, gathering her thoughts. "My mum told me that the reason I couldn't get into the Sidhe Realm is because my unconscious mind was blocking me from moving between worlds. My soul was stuck, I suppose."

Craig's forehead creased. "Do you know what was causing the block?"

The tears that she had tried to suppress ran freely over her cheeks. "My denial and guilt about my mum's death. I had buried a memory really deep to pretend it didn't happen. Basically, I was the reason she died."

"I'm sure that isn't the case, Aisling, you're just blaming yourself," said Liv.

Aisling hiccoughed. "No, it was really my fault. Since I was only a wee girl, I thought my mum had died of an epileptic seizure because of the Christmas tree lights. That's what my dad had told me happened. But she hadn't. She died of electric shock because I dropped the plug in the bowl of water under the tree."

Liv's hands flew to her face. "Oh my God, you poor thing. But you were so young, you didn't know it was dangerous."

"It doesn't matter if it was an accident or not, she's dead and it's because of me." In her anguish, Aisling's voice sounded higher and younger, much like the child she had been when her mum had been killed. Was it her unconscious mind's way of letting her inner child grieve?

"Well, that explains why you were so insistent on giving yourself an electric shock," said Eoin. "You must have wanted to punish yourself."

"I guess you're right. I was in so much denial about what happened that my body had to process it all, in some way," she said, with a sniff.

What a strange thing, denial was. Aisling thought back to the two times over the past fortnight that she had given herself electric shocks: first by the kettle and second through the fairy lights-umbrella-Newton's Cradle channel. Had it really been the stress of the season, and the repressed bad memories that had subconsciously made her want to harm herself, or worse; kill herself? She shivered.

"Well, Aisling. Maybe it's best that you rest today and gather your strength. We can resume our plan to make your spirit cross over into the Sidhe Realm another day," said Craig.

"Strangely, I already feel recharged. Unblocking that part of my mind has had a strange effect. I actually feel ready to do this – spiritually, I mean," she said.

"That makes sense." Craig set the Tree of Life book back in its position on the table. "Your psyche has been cleansed. It has been wiped clean, a blank slate. Then, if you are ready, and your friends are happy to proceed, let us try once more to send your spirit over into the Sidhe Realm."

"Yes, I'd like to." Aisling took a sip from her cup of Pixie Pear tea, feeling it work on her body, visualising her spirit drawing closer to Jimbo's.

Craig snuffed out the White Candle and replaced it with a new one. The ball bearings were still in full motion. Liv and Eoin were pale and a bit shaken, but both nodded their resolve. Aisling was grateful to have found such good friends, and in such a short space of time. It was odd to think that only two weeks before, the three of them had barely exchanged more than a few perfunctory words in lectures or tutorials, and now they were doing a séance together; a life or death task. It meant everything to Aisling. She would find a way to thank them properly, once Jimbo was found and safe.

"Aisling, I address you now individually. I ask you to focus all your powers of concentration on the Pendulum of Knowledge. Remove all other distractions from your mind. You will see only the crystal, swinging gently." Craig lifted the crystal and let go of it, setting it into a steady motion on its chain.

Aisling watched the clear crystal swinging left, then right.

"Nothing else matters, only the crystal."

The crystal. It had so many facets. Aisling tried to count them, but it was impossible. She was so sleepy.

"You can see only the crystal."

The room swirled out of focus. All the colours blended into greyish white light.

"I want you now to see the White Candle flame. It is in front of you. You will no longer see the crystal. Instead, you will see the flame. Move towards it. Follow it."

She tried to move towards the flame, but it kept the same distance ahead of her. It took her a moment to realise that she was, in fact, moving towards it but that the flame was leading her forward, making it seem like it was always out of reach.

"Keep following it. It will lead you between the worlds. In a moment, you will see a bright flash of light as you leave the real world and transition into the Sidhe Realm. I have stopped the Pendulum of Knowledge. Do you understand me? If you do, move the Pendulum."

Aisling exhaled with the effort of willing her mind: *yes, I understand.*

"Good. When you see the bright flash of light, move the Pendulum. Once you have crossed over, you may not be able to communicate any more."

Aisling drifted behind the flame. Was she walking, or floating? She couldn't feel any feet, so it was hard to say for sure. Gradually, the grey mist began to change, taking on a pale green hue. Then she could see khaki and beige tones. A bright flash of light; this had to be what Craig talked about. She channelled her mind to send another telepathic message: *I can see the flash of white light. I can see it.*

"Keep going, Aisling. You are now entering the Sidhe Realm."

Sidhe Realm. The last couple of words faded until all Aisling could hear was a static buzzing in her ear, like an untuned radio signal.

Trees were all around her; a forest. Aisling let her soul realign itself; she had made it, she was in the fairy world now, the Sidhe Realm. She could see a stream too, as Jimbo had said. Was this the stream that ran through both the Maytree in Friar's Bush and the holly in her garden back in the real world? Only here, there were no houses, no graveyard, no Botanic Gardens.

The Sidhe World wasn't full of bright colours and majesty as Aisling had imagined, it was as Jimbo had told her; a Netherworld. The tree trunks were dark brown, almost a mahogany or ebony shade and the canopy deep and shadowy. The sky above was a blanket of clouds, low slung and khaki brown in colour. The difference between this world and the physical world was stark, but Aisling was glad for the contrast; it reminded her that she wasn't in her physical body – her soul had a mission.

If this were an out of body experience, could she feel anything? Curious, Aisling moved her right leg; she lifted it up, bending it at the knee until her foot dangled. She set it down on the grass where she stood. There was a mild sensation: the spongy turf below her shoe; the pressure on the sole of her foot. It wasn't the same as in the physical world, but her spirit could sense enough in the Sidhe Realm. She was glad; the ability to sense the strange world in which she found herself was important – not only to keep her grounded, but to keep her safe.

Jimbo had said he stayed hidden in this world, as he had no friends, but many enemies. Aisling moved towards the nearest tree. It towered above her, the trunk so wide she was sure that Liv, Eoin, Craig and herself would have been able to touch fingertips around it and nothing more. She peered around the trunk and, happy that she couldn't see any movement, darted to the next tree. From there, she moved to the next, continually creeping forward.

This was easier than she thought. Aisling smiled to herself at how easy it was to stay inconspicuous. Or was it? She was a foreigner, an intruder in this realm. She didn't know the lay of the land; the Sidhe on the other hand did. What if they were staying hidden and observing her, watching what move she would make next? If they had Jimbo trapped in this world, it had to be for a very good reason. She didn't think they would welcome any rescue party coming to help him; however capable that help may be. It wasn't a comfortable notion.

Another unsettling thought popped to mind; what about Cliona? If Cliona was able to appear so clearly in the real world, unlike Jimbo who was little more than a dark shadow, what power would she wield in her own world, the Sidhe Realm? Aisling crouched lower as she crept from tree to tree, making sure to shield herself in the undergrowth too.

Jimbo, I'm here. I'm in the Netherworld. Aisling focused on each word in her mind to give it power. *I've come for you. Can you show me where you are?*

"Aisling." A whisper, a male voice. "Why did you not listen to me? Now we're both in danger."

Aisling turned to her left in the direction of a clump of bushes, where she saw Jimbo, half-concealed amidst lingering mist.

Chapter seventeen

As he moved towards her, Aisling saw him clearly for the first time. Jim Murphy was young, not more than twenty-five. He had sandy-blonde hair and a short, light brown beard. His eyes were bright green, the colour of limes. Aisling felt a pull in her chest as she came near; he was much more handsome than she had imagined. What a waste of such a young, strong life.

"You're a ghost," he said. "Oh Aisling. Did you die? Is that how you got here?"

"I'm not a ghost. My spirit managed to get here, but my body is still alive back on earth."

He pointed a wavering finger at her. "But you don't look the way you did in the real world – you're a black shadow."

Aisling looked down at her body and gasped; he was right. Her body looked like a dark outline of itself, as though her silhouette had been formed out of smoke. "I look like how you did when you appeared to me in my house."

"Something is strange. I need to help you get back into your world," he said.

"Our world," she corrected. "I came for you. You can't stay here."

"I told you already, there's no hope for me. There is no light at the end of any tunnel in this place. It's just endless drifting, the same existence, for eternity," he said, his voice sad.

What a depressing thought. "I can't believe you could feel that way. You can't simply give up? I've risked so much to come here and save you."

"And I'm thankful for that, but I'm asking you to go back to your world. Forget about me."

She looked into his sad eyes; for someone so young, there was a world-weary heaviness to them. "I can't do that. Not until your body is back in the physical world and we can give you a proper burial, in a place that will be safe from the Sidhe, where they can't touch you."

The corner of Jimbo's mouth twitched upwards. "I can see you won't listen to reason. Maybe there's a part of me that appreciates that – a big part – and admires it. I'll take you to a safe place where we can talk more without risk that they'll find us."

As they walked, Aisling noticed that silvery clouds swirled around them. At first, she thought it was their bodies churning up low-lying mist or fog in the forest, but soon realised that the clouds surrounded Jimbo; they lingered around her only because she was side by side with him. "How did you manage to get these clouds to follow you?"

"I didn't." He gave a small shrug. "They were here from the moment I arrived in this Netherworld. I've never been able to explain it. I was suspicious at first, in case it was an enchantment those others created, but I've long since gotten used to it. The clouds seem benign."

"Maybe they cling to you because you're human, not Sidhe. Our energy must be different than theirs," she said.

The clouds didn't cling to her, of course, and she was human too, but she had no other way to explain it.

Jimbo stooped as he entered a hollow inside a large tree trunk. From the outside it was concealed by thickets and other low-slung branches. As Aisling ducked to enter behind him, she noticed that the foliage had been placed deliberately in a way to hide the secret entrance. "I'm impressed. You made your own hideout."

"I like to think of it as my own anti-fairy lair," he smiled.

Inside the hollow tree trunk, Jimbo had piled leaves, feathers and ferns to make a soft, comfortable mattress on the floor. Aisling sat cross-legged and Jimbo flopped down opposite her in the cosy, dim interior.

"I suppose you used the metal implement to create a channel to get here – did you get help from the girl who gave it to you too?" said Jimbo.

Aisling lowered her head as she thought of the Newton's Cradle and Liv; two things that Jimbo had warned her to stay away from. "Yes. You guessed right. We haven't even known each other that long, yet you know me so well."

"I don't know how to create any electrical connection to send you back into the real world. My only hope now is that your friend uses the objects she has – those lights in your house and the metal implement – to summon you back," he said.

"Hope?" said a woman's voice, full of malice. "There is no hope."

Warm fingers closed around Aisling's forearm in a tight grip. Aisling reeled with the shock; she was a dark shadow in this world, yet Cliona could touch her. In a flurry of leaves and brambles from Jimbo's broken defences, Cliona's head appeared through the entrance of the hollow. Her eyes were full of wicked pleasure.

"Thanks for leading me to him. Why else do you think I was helping you get into our realm?"

"Get off me," said Aisling, trying in vain to shake Cliona off. But the ethereal being was strong; too strong.

"Run, Aisling, run! I'll hold her off." Jimbo grabbed Cliona, wrapping his arms around her to pull her off Aisling.

Aisling scampered out of the hollow tree lair. Instinct told her to run, but her rational mind overpowered her fears; she couldn't leave Jimbo. Cliona and the Sidhe wanted him, not her.

She ducked back inside in time to see Cliona on top of him, throttling him with both hands bearing down on his neck. Poor Jimbo struggled below the supernatural woman on top of him.

Aisling scanned the entrance to the hollow. If Cliona could touch her, did that mean she could touch Cliona too? She grabbed Cliona's shoulders, closing her shadow fingers around her collarbone.

"Get off him, you fiend!" Aisling pulled with all her might. Jimbo pushed Cliona off and grabbed Aisling's shadow hands within his own.

They both hurried out of Jimbo's lair. "The clouds around me should shield us until we can get far enough away from her," he said.

"I'm so sorry I got your lair discovered. She must have followed me," said Aisling.

"I'm amazed those clouds protected me for as long as they did, they must be very powerful." He flapped his hands dismissively. "But never mind that. I'll find somewhere else to hide myself once you're gone, now that she has broken through whatever spell they hold. Don't worry about me. I have taken care of myself for a long time in this Netherworld, and I'll continue to do the same. I'm dead, what worries do the dead have? You're more important – you're alive. We need to get you back to your life."

"Not without you." Aisling dug her heel into the forest floor. "I'm not going back until I find a way to bring you with me."

Jimbo sighed. "I admire your passion, but it's wasted on me. I'm dead and I'm stuck. Don't waste your youthful living essence on trying to send an old soul out of this place. It won't work."

"Ack, rubbish!" Aisling grabbed his hand and led him through the forest. "I'm going to find a way, if it's the last thing I do. I'll bring your body back to the real world to bury it and send your soul onwards into the light. Heaven help me, I'll stay here until I find that flippin' tunnel."

Jimbo laughed. "I believe you would."

Aisling didn't have time to laugh with him. At that moment, Cliona burst through the trees and brambles

114

behind them and launched herself at Aisling. Jimbo was knocked sideways in the surge of energy as Cliona rushed forward.

"You have no more purpose in this land. Be gone," Cliona spat.

Movement on all sides registered in Aisling's peripheral vision. At first, she thought the trees themselves had come alive and hurried inwards, but after a moment's recognition, she saw that a dozen Sidhe had swooped in and seized Jimbo. Now Aisling understood why she hadn't noticed them before; they were as the colour of trees. Some had mottled green skin that was pale, like a lizard's. Others had skin the colour of burnt umber, blending with the tree trunks. They had amber eyes and thin slits for pupils and their hair looked tough and fibrous, like twisted vines, or raised like antlers. The Sidhe blended perfectly in the forest, entities capable of complete camouflage.

"Let her go. Don't you harm her at all," Jimbo shouted, even as the Sidhe bound his arms with vines of the forest.

Four Sidhe grabbed Aisling's arms and legs and pinned her to the forest floor. Cliona's face appeared upside down above her own, half in shadow as she loomed over Aisling.

"I banish you back to your own world, the realm of mortals. Be gone, and come no more." Aisling felt a twig pushed into her mouth with five small berries attached. Cliona pinched her nose and covered her mouth with her hand.

Don't swallow them. Aisling concentrated. *Don't swallow them.*

Why should she swallow them? She was in the Sidhe Realm in spirit, not body. Her soul had no need to swallow or eat anything.

Aisling used her tongue to push the twig and berries out of her mouth.

Cliona dangled it above her nose and Aisling saw that it was five ripe, red holly berries on a sprig. "Swallow it, or I will force feed it to you and that would be bad – for you. Your soul would be reunited with your body, but your body would not wake up. Now, eat it."

She spat the last two words with such venom that Aisling believed her. She gulped the sprig and berries down her dry throat. A kaleidoscope of colours sprang from behind Cliona's head, a dazzling crown of light until only whiteness remained. Aisling saw nothing.

Chapter eighteen

What day was it? What time was it? Aisling blinked several times to try and stimulate any moisture as her eyes were bone dry. Her mouth was parched too. She felt as if she hadn't drank anything in days.

Her phone said it was New Year's Eve. Had she really slept for two days? She couldn't have. The last couple of days since the séance on the twenty ninth were a blur. Maybe being in the Sidhe Realm had taken more out of her psychically than she could have imagined.

She rolled her legs out of bed and let the momentum tip the rest of her body upwards too. Her feet felt like lumps of lead, thudding across the floor. How had she gotten into her pyjamas? She had no recollection of anything that had happened since Cliona had forced her out of the Sidhe Realm.

After drinking a pint of water, Aisling's senses started to return. How was it that she felt drunk and she hadn't touched a drop of alcohol? Or was it the holly berries that Cliona had force fed to her. Weren't holly berries poisonous to humans? She had a vague recollection of having had vomiting and diarrhoea so bad that she felt she had purged her body of all of its organs. That wouldn't make sense though; only her soul, not her body, had been force-fed the holly berries by Cliona to eject her spirit back to the physical world. Did that mean things in the Sidhe Realm that could harm her spirit could also harm her body in the real world?

Music sounded and Aisling enjoyed the tune for a moment before registering that it was her phone ringing. She saw Liv's face appear on the screen and answered.

"Finally, you're awake. Eoin and I have been checking on you since yesterday, but you've been out for the count."

"Checking on me?" Aisling said, her lips heavy like under the power of a dental injection.

"I held onto your key so we could get in. Hope you don't mind, but we wanted to make sure you were – not to be melodramatic or anything – alive. You know what I mean."

"Oh yeah, sure. I get it." Aisling swept her lank hair out of her face. "I'm grateful. Thanks for making sure I didn't die, or anything."

"You slept for like, sixteen hours yesterday, or something like that." Liv's voice was exasperated. "Eoin said when he popped in yesterday evening you were like a zombie, you barely even knew he was there. He got you a sandwich to eat and you didn't say anything, you just took the food and went back up to bed."

Aisling scratched her head. "I have no recollection of that at all. But there wasn't a sandwich in my room, so I guess I ate it."

"Well, I'm glad you ate something – other than those holly berries you ate during the séance."

"Holly berries?" Aisling stared at the phone screen, incredulous.

A pause. "Yeah, there was a sprig you'd left on top of your uni books over by the window. You plucked the berries off it and ate them while you were in a trance. Craig said we shouldn't stop you, because if we disturbed your body while your soul was away, it could have got lost in the Sidhe Realm forever."

At least she now had an explanation; it wasn't Cliona's holly berries in the Sidhe Realm making her physically sick, she had eaten some in real life too.

"Well anyway, at least you're well now," Liv went on. "Are you coming to Peter's party tonight? Might do you some good to get out for a bit after sleeping so much."

"Aye, sure. Text me the address and when you're heading over there and I'll make a move when you're on your way." Aisling stuck the phone in her pyjama pocket and shuffled out of the kitchen.

Searing pain shot through Aisling's head as soon as she turned on the living room light. She shut it off with a clammy hand slapped against her forehead; not that it helped. What had Cliona done to her brain? Her mind felt addled.

"Man-nah-nah-nah," Aisling mumbled. She flopped onto the sofa. "Man-nah-nan."

Yep. Definitely addled. Her brains were scrambled. Now she was uttering nonsense. Manannan. What the hell was Manannan?

Or who? She concentrated on the word. Yes; it was a name. But of who? Not a person. The name didn't sound human.

Aisling followed Craig's advice and turned off anything that caused electrical interference; all lights, Christmas LEDs and her phone. She sat in silence, emptying her mind, letting the empty void expand. Into the void came words. Memories. But not her own.

As the ice retreated from the island of Ireland, vast forests filled most of the land, sweeping over hills and valleys. Giant Irish Elk roamed the land, alongside bears and wolves. Inside the forest were beings who lived at one with the woods; they themselves had moss-green skin and eyes the colour of lichen in springtime. They had no name, for they had no need; they were the only two-legged beings on the island of Ireland.

As the climate warmed, men and women crossed on boats from the continent, along with their livestock. They cut into the forests to clear land for their roundhouses and came across the others living peaceably among the trees; the green-skins who they dubbed as the Danaan. The Danaan were the fairy folk, and the first people feared them for their wild majesty and magic.

But the first people, the Milesians, descendants of the Gauls, needed more land for their descendants – and wanted less of the Danaan in it. Aisling watched, in her mind's eye, as an epic battle unfolded where the forests themselves seemed to rise up against the threat from the Milesians. The men had swords of iron, shields of bronze sheet metal and armour – and the Danaan had bows and arrows. The Milesians ambushed them, cut into the forests with their axes, launched burning bales of hay into the forests to burn the virgin wood and claimed rule of the land. The Danaan were forced to retreat into underground mounds and became known as the Sidhe.

As the images of the Sidhe living in fairy mounds filled Aisling's mind, so too did a flood of anger and resentment: bitterness towards the Milesians. Aisling understood. This was Cliona's doing. She was seeing Cliona's memories; or those of her ancestors.

Far out in the steely waters of the Irish Sea, the God of the Sea had been watching the battle between the Milesians and the Danaan. Aisling felt his frustration and his disappointment; he had given the first people calm waters to sail across to Ireland in the hope that they would live in peace with the Danaan, and with the land itself. Now, disgruntled, he was being forced to cross the Irish Sea himself and intervene. His name came to mind: Manannan.

Manannan, God of the Sea.

Manannan stood on the shore and raised his hands to the sea. He brought forth an enchanted mist that rolled across the sand dunes and penetrated the dark forests.

Faeth Fiadha, the Cloak of Concealment.

Manannan swept the Cloak of Concealment over the Sidhe Mounds, shielding them from mortal eyes. He would give them his protection and watch over them.

But in order to look after the Sidhe, he needed to move closer. Manannan left his fortress on the Isle of

Man, in the middle of the Irish Sea and set up a new palace, closer to the fairy mounds.

"Manannan MacLir," Aisling said aloud. "And his wife, Aoife. Their palace was at Finaghy."

Finaghy. Only a stone's throw from her house with its holly bush, and the Maytree in Friar's Bush Graveyard.

"King Lir, watching over the Sidhe, from his palace at Finaghy."

The walls of her living room echoed the words back at her, giving them a prestige that maybe they deserved. This situation, of rescuing Jimbo from the Sidhe Realm, was transpiring to be a bigger endeavour than Aisling could have imagined. How on earth would she go about beating Cliona to get to him, when she didn't even know what her motive was?

*****

The pounding music made Aisling's head feel like it was reverberating. It felt like a mistake, being at this party; as an introvert with few friends, Liv's idea of letting her hair down at Peter's New Year's Eve party had seemed a good idea – in theory. All the stimulation was blocking her subconscious mind. Now that she had happened upon a nugget of information from whatever psychic connection she had managed to forge with Cliona, she wanted to hang onto that, delve into it; explore it. A bunch of drunken, noisy students from random courses, not even fellow History with Irish classmates, singing out of tune along to blaring noise from loudspeakers was hammering her head.

"Have some vodka jelly," said a random fella. Aisling looked at the glass of congealed red gloop in a tumbler that he handed her.

What the hell. It couldn't hurt. Maybe it would even lighten her up. Aisling tipped it all into her mouth in one go and let it slide down her throat. She leaned back, happy to be a wallflower, as she watched the moving figures in the room all around. Liv was chatting to a sporty-looking fella, throwing her head back as she laughed, oblivious to the reality that he was more into himself than her. Thoughts on her friend distracted her from the fact that the wall behind her was cushiony; her shoulders sank into the soft, spongy plaster.

With a gasp she jolted off the wall and turned to inspect it. She ran a hand across it. It was solid, not soft. Aisling scanned the room and spotted the fella who had given her the vodka jelly.

"Here, what did you put in this?" She gestured to the glass he had given her, now empty.

His eyes were glazed and she noticed he swayed on the spot as he tried to focus on her. "Strawberry jelly, some vodka and a wee bit of something special."

"Something special? Did you put drugs in it?" Her voice was thick and slurred.

He laughed, his eyes crinkling. "You got me. Magic mushrooms. I got them myself."

Rainbow loops arced over his head. Aisling raised her hand, a difficult effort as her arm felt like lead, and pointed to the bright colours. "I can see your aura."

"Aura? What's that?" the fella slurred back at her.

"Your soul," she said, stretching her fingers to try and catch the colours. She looked at the empty glass in her tight grip. Magic mushrooms. Cliona. "Where did you get the mushrooms?"

"You'll never guess. I got them in Friar's Bush. They were huge too, biggest I've ever seen." He leaned close, a sly glint in his eye. "All those dead bodies must give the best fertiliser."

Aisling felt bile rise in her throat and dashed upstairs to find the bathroom. She emptied the contents of her stomach in the toilet bowl and heard laughter behind, as someone snide took amusement from her misfortune. This had to be Cliona's doing. Cliona's fairy ring around the Maytree; Cliona's influence.

"Jimbo, help me. I know they've got you trapped, but you can still hear me, can't you?"

"Jimbo?" The vodka-jelly fella stood in the open doorway of the bathroom behind her. "Are you talking about Jimbo MacLir? He's a mate of mine."

"No, you wouldn't know this Jimbo." She wiped a sweaty strand of hair off her face. "Wait, what did you say? Jimbo MacLir? Where do you know him from?"

Manannan. Manannan MacLir.

"Dunno. I met him a few times in Botanic Gardens, when I was off my head. I was just sitting there with a few mates getting blocked. You know how they have the Christmas lights on the pine trees, and all? Well, he appeared under them, out of nowhere."

Her heart beat faster as he talked. "What did he look like, this Jimbo MacLir?"

A distant expression came over his face. "Lemme see. He was shadowy, so I couldn't see him well in the darkness."

A shadowy form that appeared because of the fairy lights on the trees.

It had to be the same Jimbo, the description was the same. But what about the name? Jimbo was Jim Murphy, not Jimbo MacLir. Could it be a coincidence?

There was no way Jimbo was a distant relative of the mythical figure from Celtic folklore, Manannan the God of the Sea? Was there?

Chapter nineteen

"I'm surprised you were able to get a delivery so soon after New Year." Liv gestured at the brown cardboard box on Aisling's living room floor.

Aisling opened the box and lifted out an L-shaped object covered in bubble wrap. She unrolled the wrapping and held in her hands two copper rods that were lightweight and sturdy. They were bigger than she had imagined from the images online, a foot long with cylindrical handles that slotted well in each palm.

"What're those prongs for?" Eoin nodded at them, his face puzzled.

"They're dowsing rods." Aisling gripped the handle of each rod and manoeuvred the end of each one inwards until they were almost touching. She felt a pull, almost like a magnetic force, as the ends responded to each other.

"You mean those things that detect hidden sources of water?" said Eoin.

"Aye, pretty much. They can also pick up on ley lines, places of spiritual energy that run across the country."

"How do you know all this?" Liv ran her finger along one of the copper rods then withdrew her hand as though she'd received an electric shock.

"I'm still connected to Cliona's knowledge, that's how. I'm not even sure if she's aware how much I've been able to see and feel through her thoughts and memories. I've seen the river running through the Sidhe Realm. They're holding Jimbo prisoner along its banks. If I can find out more about it, I can locate it, and save Jimbo."

"Then I suppose you should get going on trying to find out what you can before she realises and cuts off the connection," said Eoin.

"Or worse – tries to kill you," Liv added.

Not the most reassuring thoughts, but it was better to treat both notions as realistic possibilities that might happen. "Alright, let's do this."

Eoin held the front door open and Liv locked it behind them using Aisling's latch key, allowing Aisling to keep both hands on the dowsing rods. Was it like a séance, where you had to keep your hands linked at all times or you broke the connection? She wasn't sure, but time was of the essence, so she didn't want to take the risk of losing any progress. Of course, that was if anything were to happen. So far apart from the initial magnetic pull of the two ends drawn to each other, nothing had happened with the rods.

Aisling stepped out of her garden, and the rods lurched to the left, both at a ninety degree angle to her stomach. The sensation made her gasp; energy from the ethereal world was stronger than she was expecting.

As she walked, Aisling felt as though the physical world was falling away from her. In reality it remained all around her like normal, but she visualised it as a transparent layer lying over another dimension; the real world began to fade like an old photograph and the dense woodland of the Sidhe Realm emerged all around.

"We're walking through a forest. I know this part, I've been here before. This is where I arrived when Craig helped me pass over," she said.

Liv pushed her way in between Eoin and Aisling, looking behind and in front with fear on her face. "We're not going to get attacked by any fairies, are we?"

"No, the dowsing rod is showing me the lay of the land, that's all. I'm the only one who can see it," Aisling reassured her.

They turned the corner at the bottom of the street and started walking towards Botanic Gardens.

"Can you actually see any Sidhe yourself, even if we can't?" Eoin's voice wavered; seemed that he too, like Liv, was afraid.

"Not so far, but they're good at hiding. Even when my spirit was fully in their realm it took a while for any to show themselves."

Aisling walked towards a small, low lying tree with wide splayed branches, bare of all its leaves in the physical realm. In the Sidhe Realm, she saw the tall, wide trunk of the tree with a hollow where Jimbo had hidden from his fairy enemies for a century. With a stab of guilt, Aisling thought of how her presence had alerted Cliona to his hideout and had led to his capture. In one afternoon, she had endangered the safety of a soul that had successfully stayed secret for one hundred years.

She swallowed her guilt and followed the direction the dowsing rods pointed. They veered left towards Friar's Bush Graveyard as she expected and when she followed the turn, they swung straight in front, allowing her to follow the unseen river.

"He's nearby, I'm sure of it," said Aisling.

As if in response, the dowsing rods fell apart as no more magnetic pull held the ends together.

"Did you lose the connection?" said Liv.

She sucked in a large lungful of air, then blew it out through the gap in her teeth. "No. It's because of the clouds. There are clouds that surround Jimbo. I'm guessing they hide the water around him too, which must be why the dowsing rods can't detect it. The clouds stop him from being seen by the Sidhe in their realm. Well, at least they did until I led Cliona right to him and he got captured."

Faeth Fiadha. Cloak of Concealment.

The words floated back to her on a memory. No; Cliona's memory. Manannan, God of the Sea, shielded the Sidhe from mortal eyes by the Cloak of Concealment. Now, concentrated remnants of Faeth Fiadha surrounded Manannan's last descendent: Jim Murphy.

Aisling pointed beyond the perimeter wall of Friar's Bush Graveyard, where the backs of houses on Landseer Street sat in a row, their pointed rooftops casting a looming shadow across the headstones. "He's over there. They're holding him on the banks of the river just where you can see that alleyway behind the houses."

Silence fell between the three of them. Aisling wondered if Eoin and Liv were thinking the same thing: how would they get inside a gated alleyway? In an ideal situation, they would hold another séance on that spot and Aisling would cross over into the Sidhe Realm right beside Jimbo to rescue him.

Aisling looked back at the Maytree. "I have no other choice. The Maytree has the strongest connection to the Sidhe Realm in this graveyard. I'll have to cross over into their world underneath its branches. Though that doesn't bode well for Jimbo, as they'll see me coming straight away, so rescuing him might be over and done with before I even have a chance to get started."

"What were you thinking in terms of a rescue plan?" said Eoin.

Aisling turned her palms up, at a loss. "I hadn't thought it through, to be fair. I had hoped to grab him and get him out of there, somehow, into this world and maybe use Craig to send him on into the light."

Come to me.

"Cliona?" said Aisling aloud, even though she knew the words were in her head. She stared at the trunk of the Maytree, the direction from which the voice came.

The fairy ring still surrounded the Maytree trunk, the mushrooms bright white in the midday light. An image formed in her mind: a handsome, blonde-haired man sitting on the grass with his back against the twisted tree trunk, in the midst of the fairy ring. He wore a linen shirt, rolled up at the sleeves and closed his eyes as the bright, Mayday sunshine warmed his face.

Have something to eat. Yes, she was sure. Cliona.

Cliona was speaking to Jimbo, not her.

"Yes, that does sound rather nice," said Jimbo. He plucked a mushroom from the grass, rubbed it on his shirt and ate it whole, followed by another. Then another. Soon he had eaten the whole fairy ring.

Wash it down with a drink. Cliona's voice, smooth as belladonna.

Jimbo spotted a wooden beaker in the grass near his left shoulder. He raised the cup to his lower lip. It had to be Pixie Pear tea, same as Cliona had given to her. Aisling watched, helpless to intervene, as Jimbo washed down the mushrooms with Pixie Pear tea. It was only a memory, Cliona's memory, of an event that had already taken place. Would she witness Jimbo's death, under the Maytree? She herself had drunk Pixie Pear tea – but not eaten any of the mushrooms from Cliona's fairy ring. Was it poison to consume both at once? Aisling stared hard with her inner eye witnessing the scene with her heart in her throat.

Jimbo's head began to loll against the Maytree trunk. His eyelids grew heavy and flickered shut. Drool ran from his open mouth. As his body slumped lower in the grass, Aisling wondered if her eyes were deceiving her. He seemed to be disappearing into the twisted tree roots, as though the gnarled wood parted and swallowed him up. The flaky bark splintered around his shoulders, creeping across his arms and the hawthorn leaves closed over his chest, like snaking vines pulling his body into the trunk. She stared, transfixed in horror, until his legs and feet disappeared; the Maytree had entirely consumed him and she found herself looking at the plain trunk.

"Oh my God."

She blinked, allowing her surroundings to reappear, including her friends. Liv and Eoin's faces were etched with concern – and confusion.

"Jimbo," she gasped.

"What is it? Have they done something to him?" said Eoin.

Aisling's heart hammered in her chest. She clapped a hand against it and felt the gentle rise and fall of her chest with each breath, grounding herself in the moment so her body would centre itself and rebalance. In and out, inhale, exhale, thinking only of the present. The past was too overwhelming, too much to absorb.

"I can't take it in, what happened. I saw him. I saw Jimbo in the past, a hundred years ago. Cliona lured him into the Sidhe Realm."

"You mean, like, she lured his ghost from this graveyard into the fairy world?" said Liv.

"No." Aisling concentrated on the spot where Jimbo had sat a century before, as though the imprint of him gave her strength. "See that's the thing. I don't think he was dead. I think he was alive when they got him."

"Wow, that's messed up." Eoin's eyes were glassy as he stared off across the graveyard. "They killed him in their world."

"I'm not even sure if Jimbo knows. I think he thought he was already dead when they stole his corpse."

Aisling's mind turned from thoughts of physical to metaphysical spaces. In spirit form, she had encountered significant challenges crossing over into another dimension; what about Jimbo crossing over not only in spirit form, but as a whole flesh and blood person? Did he die in the process? Or what if—

Her heart jumped to her throat.
What if Jimbo wasn't dead?

Chapter twenty

Knock knock knock. Bang bang bang.
Who the hell was being so rude as to bang at the front door in such a manner?

"Take the door off the hinges, why don't you, you bloody demon?" Aisling huffed. But even as she hurried downstairs laden with her fairy lights in one hand and the golf umbrella in the other, she could see through the frosted glass panel that Craig, the psychic, stood on her doorstep. Liv and Eoin joined her in the hallway, peering towards the front door.

She pulled the door wide. "Craig, what is it?"

"I have a message from your Mum. She said to stop what you're about to do," he said, his arms outstretched to beseech her.

"Did she tell you what I'm planning?"

He shook his head in a theatrical manner. "Only that what you're planning is reckless and could kill you. She doesn't want you to do it – she doesn't think Jimbo would either."

Aisling thought of Jimbo, held prisoner and surrounded by the clouds of his *Faeth Fiadha*. "I have to. I found out some more things since we did the séance. The reason he's so valuable to them is that he's a descendent of Manannan MacLir himself – the God of the Sea in Celtic belief. Don't you see? He's part deity. Jimbo isn't dead. He's alive over in the Sidhe Realm – the Sidhe are holding him prisoner."

Craig looked like he was going to vomit. "That's impossible. That can't be. Only spirits can pass through into other planes of existence."

"Cliona did it. She's behind it all. I've been connecting to her thoughts and memories," said Aisling.

Craig gave a solemn nod. "I know. I did some research of my own in the days since we held our séance. I found out who she is."

Craig's mouth moved as he talked, but Aisling didn't hear his words. She didn't need to. She already knew who Cliona was. An image of Cliona, with her birch tree white skin and yellow eyes the colour of lichen, floated before her, full of smashing good looks and devastating charm.

"Cliona was once the goddess of love and beauty, but she fell from grace," said Aisling. "She spent her days luring sailors to drown at sea, but when she fell for a handsome man, Keevan of the Curling Locks, while he was fishing one day, Manannan the God of the Sea took his chance while she was distracted and swept her out into the Irish Sea. When she washed ashore, she found herself trapped in the Sidhe Realm, where she took her throne as Queen of the Banshees."

"Oh my God, Aisling. Your mum is right. Maybe you shouldn't go up against the Queen of the Banshees. Now that you know who she is, shouldn't you stop?" said Liv, her face flushed.

What a killjoy Liv could be; the first sign of danger and she was checking out. "And leave Jimbo over there, alive and trapped? Never. What sort of person would I be if I didn't at least try to save him?"

Craig closed his eyes, a meditative look on his face. "I have a feeling that nothing would stop her, so we should at least help in giving her a fighting chance."

Aisling smiled at him, glad that he was at last talking sense. "You're right. I have a plan, something that I think might have a snowball's chance in hell of working. But I need you all to be in with me. Are you with me, or out?"

"In," said Craig with confidence.

"Same here," said Eoin.

Liv cast a furtive glance at each of them. "Me too."

"That's dead on." Aisling paused to appreciate the moment; three people, who barely knew her, but were placing their trust in her. Her chest swelled. "So, basically, my idea is for us all to spread out to points that the dowsing rods showed me are connected in the Sidhe Realm. Craig and I will go to the Maytree in Friar's Bush Graveyard, along with the fairy lights and the dowsing rods."

"Ah, I'm guessing that's to provide an electrical connection?"

"Yes. The fairy lights will help to send me across – body and spirit – into the Sidhe Realm." She slotted three AA batteries into the case, while it was on her mind.

"And what about me?" said Liv.

"I need you to sit in my front garden with your back against the holly bush and hold the Newton's Cradle in your lap."

Liv wrinkled her nose. "Won't I get prickled?"

Aisling tried to cover her exasperation. "Not bare-skinned, you'll have your coat on. When the time comes, the ball bearings next to the holly bush will be my first signal that Jimbo and I are on the right track."

"What's my job? Do I stay with her?"

"No, Eoin, you're going to go to my uncle's house in Finaghy."

Eoin recoiled in horror. "You mean, the house where your mum got killed?"

"Yes, she got killed there, but she won't harm you."

Eoin didn't look convinced; at least his face didn't relax. But he gave a solemn nod regardless. "What do I have to do?"

"Stand next to the Christmas tree in Uncle Gerry's living room with the golf umbrella open above your head. I've thought it through. He always puts the tree back up after our family gathering on Boxing Day, and the connection will be strong there as mum is my spirit guide, so she'll be attracted to that spot. The golf umbrella beside the Christmas tree should send the second signal that'll help guide Jimbo and I back into this world."

"Will your uncle be alright with that?" Eoin still looked wary.

Aisling flapped her hand. "He's an easy-going man, he'll be grand with it."

"And how will we know it's working?" said Liv.

"I'll send you a sign. Look out for something that makes you think of me," said Aisling.

***

Aisling sat on her haunches inside the fairy ring. Craig sat facing her looking much more serene in a lotus position. The wide ring of bright, white mushrooms accommodated both of them, though it was a snug squeeze with their legs almost touching.

"I've learned so much in the past four days, since we did our séance. There were passages in the book of life that I didn't understand, but they've become clear to me," said Craig.

"Like what?" she said, curious.

"About the seven planes of existence, or consciousness, if you like. The first plane is the inorganic realm, a place of dark shadows that encompasses the rocks, soil and minerals in earth's most basic, raw form."

"The Shadow World. I've been there before – when I electrocuted myself my soul ended up there, but Cliona found me," said Aisling.

"The second plane is the realm of organic material – plants and trees. This is the Sidhe Realm, as magical beings are attracted to its natural environment. Our world, the third plane of existence is the realm of protein-based lifeforms. It is the physical world, a place of pain – and pleasure – of the flesh. Above this is the fourth plane of spirits. This is where our astral selves go after death from the third, physical plane."

"I think I've been there too. It's where I met my mum when I got lost during the séance." Aisling wiped a tear with her pinky finger. "It's where I found out about my part in her death – or unblocked it from my subconscious."

"Possibly. When we have an out of body experience, we can sometimes find ourselves there if we stray too far from the third plane, our physical world. Likewise, spirits in the fourth plane can move freely into the lower realms and back to their own, though they need good cause to go there. The universal laws bind most souls to their correct plane of consciousness according to the vibrations they emit."

Aisling thought of her mum, forever young in the astral dimension, the fourth plane. It was a happy thought to think of her there.

"The fifth plane is one of orbs, where spirits who ascend and become masters of their souls shed the form they took on earth and become spheres of light. These souls emit higher vibrations that morph into pure energy."

"How does a soul become a master?" said Aisling.

"By connecting with the unconscious mind and binding all knowledge from our former lifetimes. Once we overcome obstacles from a former incarnation on earth, we learn from those mistakes and we emit higher vibrations."

"Can a person who is still alive reach the fifth dimension – or beyond – during an out of body experience?"

Craig inhaled, his nostrils flaring as he pondered her question. "There have been one or two known cases in parapsychology where people who hadn't died managed to reach the fifth plane and return. It is theoretically possible for an earthly soul to reach the sixth plane too, a realm of rainbows where the laws of time and space themselves reside. Here, spirits are separated into the individual fibres of their consciousness. If they are ready, orbs here transcend above to the seventh and final plane on their journey of higher consciousness, or they return to the third plane for another earthly journey. The sixth plane is the last place where evil can reside too."

Aisling imagined the sixth plane, a higher metaphysical realm with the fabric of the universe all around and souls stripped into the colours of the rainbow, like light through a glass prism. The very thought filled her mind with beauty; and courage for her own journey which she would soon undertake into the second plane of existence, the Sidhe Realm.

"The seventh plane is where the universal energy from which everything is derived resides. It is the source of all that is and will ever be. It is light in its purest form. It is the energy that makes up the protons, neutrons and electrons that form the nucleus of an atom. No evil resides in the seventh plane, only energy."

"Energy can neither be created nor destroyed, only converted from one form into another," said Aisling, thinking of the Newton's Cradle.

"Yes, that's right," Craig smiled. "The Law of Conservation of Energy."

Aisling felt less frightened and more heartened about her journey. It was less scary to think that no matter what happened to her physical self, her spirit would survive, whether to move on to the fourth plane of spirits, or to linger in the lower planes of existence: the Shadow World, the Sidhe Realm or remain on earth as a ghost.

"I have a question." She took a deep breath. "If there are universal laws that govern where souls have to stay – according to their energy vibration – then how did a living man from the third plane on earth manage to go to a lower existence such as the Sidhe Realm, which is the second plane?"

"A good question." Craig arched his back in a yogic pose. "I suppose it's because Cliona is a fallen goddess. She is originally of a higher dimension – most likely the sixth plane. I'm assuming she used some of her own higher energy to manipulate the laws of time and space to ensure that Jim Murphy was able to live, in his flesh form, in the Sidhe Realm. You did say that Jimbo himself is part deity, am I right?"

"Yes, he's the last living descendant of Manannan MacLir, the Celtic God of the Sea," she said.

"If that is the case, then he would have the higher energy needed to survive in the second plane without harm," said Craig.

Faeth Fiadha: the Cloak of Concealment. No wonder the Sidhe couldn't find him until Cliona did. His energy was more powerful than theirs, even in their own plane of existence.

Aisling looked up at the iron grey sky. She looked down at the brown patchy mid-winter grass. She felt the wind in her hair, smelled the fresh scent of salty tidal air blowing in off the River Lagan. She was safe. She was grounded.

"I'm ready to do this. I'm ready to go and rescue Jimbo, come what may," she said.

Chapter twenty-one

Maybe it was the mushrooms. Maybe it was the Pixie Pear tea. Maybe it was both. Or what if it was the dowsing rods, with the sprig of holly on one end and hawthorn on the other? Or, could it be the fairy lights, glowing in her pocket.

Maybe it was all of those things at once.

Aisling was no expert. What she did know was that she couldn't feel her body. Was she still sitting on her haunches, opposite Craig, on the grass? Was she standing? Flying?

The ground fell away as she floated upwards, engulfed by white light.

"Something's different this time, Craig. There's no darkness or shadows. It's all white." Aisling heard her voice in her mind, but knew she wasn't speaking; it was a mere telepathic projection.

Light. A light at the end of the tunnel. Could she be dead? Had the combination of mushrooms and Pixie Pear tea killed her? But no; she thought the same recipe had killed Jimbo, yet he remained alive in the Sidhe Realm.

If she wasn't dead and she wasn't having an out of body experience, then the only other possibility was that Cliona's concoction had succeeded in sending both her body and mind across into one of the other planes of consciousness; hopefully the second plane, the Sidhe Realm, for Jimbo's sake.

The brightness hurt her eyes. The longer she stared at the whitish-grey all around, the more it seemed to have a pink undertone, much like the sky before heavy rain. Soon the pink became purple, then blue. Craig had told her during the séance that she would see a bright flash of light as she transitioned across from the third plane of existence, the physical world, into the second plane of existence, the Sidhe Realm.

Aisling looked down at her body. When her spirit had entered the Sidhe Realm before, during the séance, she had been a shadow form. This time her body looked as it did back in the physical realm, the third plane of existence.

"I made it across. I'm alive," she gasped.

Time to get a grip though; she had a job to do. With shaking hands, Aisling gripped the handles of the dowsing rods and touched the copper ends so that the sprigs of holly and hawthorn were touching. The rods swung to the right. She followed them and soon saw the river, flowing between the trees. It was fast-flowing, though only about five feet wide.

"Jimbo, don't worry, I'm coming," she said in a whisper.

Without warning, the dowsing rods fell apart in the same way they had before in Friar's Bush Graveyard when she had tested them. It was a sure sign that Jimbo was near; only the Cloak of Concealment could have such an effect. She tucked the handles into the back waistband of her trousers, feeling the cold metal of the copper rods against her back and the prickle of the holly sprig through her clothing. The discomfort was a stark reminder that she was alive, not a spirit, and needed to stay grounded if she were to be successful in her mission.

Aisling stayed on the riverbank, following its course. How long had she been walking? When she and Jimbo had been pursued before, it hadn't taken that long before Cliona caught up with them and seized Jimbo. This time it felt like she had been walking for miles. Could it be because this time her physical self was in the Sidhe Realm, making bodily sensations more unpleasant than her free floating spirit? Or could it be that the atmosphere in the second plane of existence seemed much more dense than on earth? Walking certainly seemed like much more effort than in the real world, as though the force of gravity were stronger. Who knew?

"Jimbo, if you can hear me, give me a sign," she telepathed.

The river widened as she walked. It was comparable now to the mouth of the River Lagan, where it flowed into Belfast Lough. Aisling stopped walking as her eyes rested on a crannog in the middle of the water. She could see the thatched, conical rooftop above the trees that surrounded it. The perimeter of the circular island was lined with thick wooden posts.

"You're there, aren't you Jimbo? That's where they're holding you." Her words floated on a breathy whisper across the river.

The crannog didn't seem to be connected to the riverbank; it was on its own unattached island. How would she get across? She wasn't the best swimmer. As she wracked her brain to think of a way over, ripples lapped at the muddy bank and Aisling saw a boat sail towards her.

Holly will keep me safe. Holly will ward them off. Aisling repeated the words in her mind, a mantra, giving her courage. There was no other way that she could think of other than a confrontation if she were to rescue Jimbo. Two Sidhe grew ever nearer, their skin mint-green and watching her with eyes the colour of lichen. The first one's hair looked like tufts of dark green heather that grew on peat bogs, the other had long, stringy hair that resembled deep, red dulse. It put her in mind of her grandfather who had loved to eat dulse, the local seaweed, on trips to Bangor when she was a child. The physical differences between humans and these fairy folk was stark; a welcome reminder that she needed to be careful in this unusual and unpredictable world.

"You, come with us. We have what you want," said the one at the prow of the boat. The fairy gestured in a harsh, sharp way, but a manner that she understood, nonetheless. The language it spoke sounded like an uncommon, colloquial dialect of Irish, but she found that she understood it. This was the language of the Milesians, the first Gaels in Ireland, a precursor of the Irish language.

"Have you harmed Jimbo?" The words flowed out of her mouth with an air of confident authority that she didn't know she had in her.

"Nothing permanent," it said.

Aisling climbed into the boat, unsurprised that neither of the two fairies moved to help her. They made room for her in the middle and though she wasn't bound by rope, Aisling knew she was a prisoner. Why did she feel like she was being ferried across the River Styx by Charon, the ferryman of death? She suppressed the unwelcome thought.

The ride was smooth, the water calm and black beneath the boat. Aisling peered over the side and saw her reflection in the glassy water. The ease of her expression gave her a boost. Why was she so confident? Fear would have been a more likely response; yet here she was, looking smug. It made no sense. She had no plan. Not only that but she was in a hostile world with enemies all around; agents of Cliona who intended harm for her, and for Jimbo.

I am safe. I am grounded. Holly will keep me safe. Holly will ward them off.

Holly. The mantra reminded her of the dowsing rods. She no longer felt the cold metal on her back, or the prickly sprig pushing through her clothing. Aisling reached behind her back; they were gone.

She turned and looked back at the land falling away behind as they sailed towards the crannog. There, lying in the mud of the riverbank, were the two dowsing rods. They must have fallen out of the back waistband of her trousers when she climbed into the boat.

Dumb. So dumb and careless! How could she have forgotten to check for such an important item; so important that it was essentially her amulet in an unfamiliar and strange realm. Beads of moisture broke out across her hairline, her confidence ebbing on the tide of sweat.

"Why did you come back here? Cliona sent you away the last time you came into our realm?" The second Sidhe jabbed its knuckle into Aisling's back as the boat bumped ashore and she rose.

Aisling climbed over the side onto a short, wooden jetty. "Because Cliona doesn't dictate to me whether I come here or stay away. Jimbo is my friend and I don't intend to leave here without him."

"Cliona will decide whether you leave here or not – and whether you do so alive or dead," said the first Sidhe.

So they knew she was alive. Aisling had been hoping that fact hadn't been detected; it could have been the ace up her sleeve. Oh well. Not that she had a plan in the first place. Maybe having a blank canvas was her best approach to outsmarting Cliona and the Sidhe at any rate; certainly the only option she had. Did it stand in her favour that she was a living being from the third plane of existence, a higher dimension, than the Sidhe – even in their own realm?

The two Sidhe wedged her between themselves and frogmarched her through the ring of trees surrounding the edge of the crannog and into a clearing. The circular roundhouse that she had seen from the riverbank, poking above the canopy, was even more impressive up close. It was palatial in size for a wooden dwelling and could have filled the Ulster Museum, overlooking Friar's Bush Graveyard in the real world. The walls were wattle and daub covering what she presumed were wooden posts. The thatched roof stretched at least four storeys high. It had to be Cliona's palace, though it looked to be straight out of the Bronze Age; something that Aisling had only seen reconstructed once when she had visited the Ring of Gullion.

Aisling was surprised when her captors led her around the outside of the gigantic roundhouse towards the back; she had convinced herself that Cliona would have held Jimbo in the largest, most impressive abode, considering that he was a descendant of Manannan MacLir. Instead she saw a timber henge erected at the rear of the roundhouse palace. It consisted of twelve wooden posts hewn from the thick, dark tree trunks she had seen in the forest. She guessed the wooden henge was about thirty feet in diameter. Standing in the middle with their backs to her were Cliona and two Sidhe, flanking her on either side. Their heads were bowed as though in prayer.

Strange, overpowering incense met them as Aisling approached with her two captors. Her head swam and she turned to breathe fresh air over her shoulder from a gust channelling across the river. It was only as she drew nearer that she saw why Cliona and the two Sidhe flanking her were looking down. They weren't in prayer as she had thought; they stared into a circular pit that had been dug in the earth. The pit was lined by wooden staves and fastened with what looked like bronze, or iron rivets; Aisling was no expert. Aisling approached the edge and peered in. It had to be around ten feet deep. Jimbo was at the bottom, slumped against one side.

"Aisling," Jimbo slurred. His eyes were bleary and his voice slow and dull; probably a combination of the incense and whatever Cliona had given him to subdue him. Mushrooms? Hawthorn? Another concoction that Cliona had conjured. Possibly the same fate lay in store for her too.

"You can join him willingly or by force. The choice is yours," said Cliona.

"I came here of my own free will, so nobody will lay a hand on me." Aisling crouched down, ready to climb inside the pit.

Chapter twenty-two

Free will was well and good. Confidence was well and good. But where did good intentions get her? She would soon be a prisoner of Cliona, just as Jimbo was, with no holly to ward of the fairies and no dowsing rods to help them navigate away from danger. Such dour thoughts flooded her mind as she sat down at the edge of the wooden pit, dangling her feet inside. It was only a ten foot drop, by her estimation. Aisling flipped her body around, so that her stomach was flat again against the ground and slithered backwards, grasping the wooden rim with her fingertips. She hung inside the pit for a second before releasing her grip and dropping. As her feet struck the base, her ankle twinged and she keeled backwards until she lay, sprawled in the middle of the pit.

"Aisling, this is no good. Get away before you lose all sense of yourself," Jimbo slurred.

Aisling didn't have to ask why. Ten incense sticks were wedged between the wooden slats, each one placed in alignment with the timber posts of the henge that encircled them. Instead of the smoke blowing upwards, as she would have expected, the fragrant air burning from the end of each tip pooled downwards into the pit, creating a shimmering mist around them both.

"I'm not leaving without you," she said, an edge of heaviness already in her voice.

"It's too late for me. Don't wait until it's too late for you too," he added.

Anger bubbled up through Aisling's core, sudden and unexpected, clearing her head. "Ack, nonsense. You're such a defeatist. The way you talk, you'd think we're dead already. Hope isn't lost."

Jimbo was crestfallen. He lowered his eyes then hung his head in shame. Guilt flooded Aisling. What good did reprimanding him do? If he was too weak to help, she would think of a plan to save them both. She just had to think of how to outsmart Cliona.

What could she do to outsmart Cliona?

Aisling turned to the Queen of the Banshees. What was a banshee, but a harbinger of death? So, Cliona planned to kill them; that much was obvious. They had both arrived, alive in the Sidhe Realm, making her job easy. It was clear that Cliona had destined them to die. But why?

"Are we being offered as a sacrifice?" Aisling mustered as much confidence as she could; show no signs of weakness to the enemy.

"It is necessary," came Cliona's clipped response.

"Necessary for what? Is it something we can negotiate about?"

Cliona stared down her nose at Aisling in the pit. "Don't you find it curious that you weren't able to see my thoughts on why it's necessary? Didn't you find that strange when I showed you so much else?"

Showed; so everything Aisling had seen through Cliona's memories had been deliberate. Cliona had orchestrated it all. Aisling felt foolish; how she should have known!

"Alright, I get it. You didn't show me why it's necessary. So, why tell me about it now?"

"Why not? You're in my sacrificial pit. You can't escape. You're no threat to me," Cliona snorted.

Best to play Devil's advocate; what other plan did she have? "I really don't see how killing Jimbo and me will do anything for you."

"That's where you're wrong." Cliona paused, licking her lips. "Do you remember how I came to be in the Sidhe Realm?"

Aisling searched Cliona's memories that seemed to have filled half her brain. "You were a goddess, in one of the higher planes of existence. But you fell from grace. You ended up in the third realm – earth – where you were seduced by a mortal man known as Keevan of the Curling Locks. While you were distracted by him, you were swept away into the sea by Manannan MacLir, and you found yourself washed up here, in the second plane of existence."

"Let's see you put your wee brain to some use, in that case. If you were me, why do you think I would sacrifice the pair of you? What good would it do me?" Cliona's spoke in a cloying, sing-song manner. The Queen of the Banshees delighted in toying with her prey, it seemed. Aisling was happy for her to bide her time; the more information she could get, the better equipped she would be if there were to be any chance of escape.

"Jimbo is the descendant of Manannan MacLir, the god who put you and the Sidhe in this realm. It's only natural that you would want to sacrifice him in revenge," said Aisling.

"Clever girl," Cliona teased.

"I'm guessing then that if Jimbo dies, you get to leave this realm permanently – his life in exchange for your own," Aisling continued.

Cliona's lip curled into a derisive smirk. "Well done. Now, aren't you the smart cookie then?"

"I suppose that means if you sacrifice me too, you can release one of your Sidhe along with you – am I right?" Aisling looked at the two fairies flanking Cliona. "Ah, but that wouldn't be fair, would it? Which one would you pick?"

The two Sidhe on either side of her made no reaction, each watching her with the same unchanging, intense glare. What a disappointment; she had hoped to cause dissent, maybe even jealousy and suspicion between them, each against the other. Cliona had them better trained than Aisling gave her credit for.

"I can't really see how a plain and simple mortal girl like myself is any use to you though? I'm not a descendant of any god or other immortal." Aisling flapped a hand. "Then again, you seem to have a soft spot for mortals, don't you? Is that how Keevan swept you off your feet? Or should I say, swept you into sea and out of the third plane of existence?"

This time, Cliona's smug face crumpled into one of fury and for a split second, Aisling swore she saw the

Banshee Queen's eyes glow yellow with hatred. She grinned to herself; Cliona had a few buttons she could push, after all.

"You can talk all you want, it won't make any difference to your fate. Once your mortal body dies in this realm, I will be released from here and free to travel to higher dimensions once more – not only in spirit, but in body too."

Aisling looked again at the incense sticks. Maybe it was adrenaline coursing through her, but her head had cleared of all its fogginess caused by their smoke. Jimbo, on the other hand had succumbed to a stupor; his eyes were shut and his head lolled on his chest.

"Jimbo?" Aisling crouched down and put her ear to his nose and mouth. Warm air tickled her cheek. He was alive. She stood upright against and faced Cliona. "If your plan is to kill us by smoke inhalation, I'm afraid to break the bad news to you – it's not going to work."

In the absence of both her anger and smugness, Cliona now looked bored. "You'll find out soon enough how you are to be sacrificed. It'll be one of two ways. I myself can't wait to see what will come first. Ah – wait just a moment. We've just got our answer."

Cliona clapped her hands together once, in a wide, theatrical gesture of delight. Aisling craned her neck to see what was coming. An onslaught of armed Sidhe, ready to stab them to death with spears? Lightning bolts from the heavens? Another, even more dramatic and dangerous death?

A trickling noise followed by a soft, splashing sound drew her attention. Water was beginning to pour into the pit. Aisling watched the wood where it pooled turn a darker shade of brown as it absorbed the trickle. Soon the wood became saturated and the water collected on top as a puddle.

"You intend to drown us," said Aisling.

"Aww, I really thought you would have got that quicker, how disappointing," Cliona scolded.

"Mannanan MacLir swept you out to sea so now you're going to drown his descendant by sea water." Aisling visualised the water rising from the river surrounding the crannog. It had to be a tidal river, like its counterpoint on earth: the River Lagan.

"So, Jimbo and I are to remain trapped here and wait to die," said Aisling.

"It would've been much more serene for you, if only you would stop talking and let the incense dull your senses. I'm not sadistic, you know. I was once known as the goddess of beauty and love. Your death could have been harmonious." Cliona waved her hand, wafting the smoke towards Aisling.

Aisling sat down beside Jimbo. Trying to escape by climbing out seemed futile; Cliona plus the two Sidhe who flanked her, not to mention the other two Sidhe who had ferried her across to the crannog, outnumbered Jimbo and herself. That was besides the fact Jimbo was incapacitated. There was no way she could haul him over her shoulder in a fireman's lift and try and escape anywhere; it wasn't going to happen.

She needed to use her mind to find a means of escape.

Her mind; of course.

Cliona wanted to kill her, body and mind. Body and mind, mind and body; true death could only be achieved if both were eliminated from a plane of existence *at the same time*. In order to thwart Cliona's plan, she had to separate her spirit from her physical self once more; to induce an out of body experience.

But how? Aisling rested her head against the wooden side of the pit, as the water rushed over her toes. Think. She had to think. She shoved her hands in her pockets as her mind worked quicker than the rising tide, and her fingers crunched against a hard bundle. Aisling pulled out a fistful of tangled wire and glass bulbs.

The fairy lights!

She had put the fairy lights into her pocket, after inserting batteries, before she had left with Craig to go to Friar's Bush Graveyard.

Aisling looked down at the swirling water around her ankles. With her right thumb, she flicked the switch, turning on the fairy lights. With her left hand, she unravelled the ball of wire and dropped the battery case into the water. She squeezed two bulbs between the finger and thumb of each hand, pinching the glass until she heard the faint pop as each broke.

Water, plus electricity meant–

Pain. A zapping noise. Bright lights and a tremor in her chest. Her heart splintered into a thousand butterflies in her chest. Her mind rose higher, catching the wind, and was gone.

Chapter twenty-three

"Aisling, honey, follow me. Come this way."

"Mum? Where are you?"

Everything was white-washed. Did that mean she had transitioned through into another realm? It was as though she were floating in a pearly white pool; or clear water with bright light shining from above. Her arms certainly moved with a thickness as though she were swimming in water. She couldn't feel ground below her feet either.

"I can't see you, mum. Can you see me?"

"Your eyes aren't adjusted to this place yet, that's all. Give it a few minutes."

Her mum was right. As she acclimatised, Aisling could see glittering spheres floating. Their gentle, luminescent beauty sent light zigzagging across an unusual, silvery landscape. Rounded hills the colour of pearls, gave way to deep curved canyons, opalescent in hue, and the strange, shining orbs drifted hither and thither among them. There was no sun, moon or stars in the metallic sky above; all light emanated from the spheres.

As Aisling turned to take in the landscape, her mum's appearance standing directly behind caused her to jump.

"You scared the life out of me." Aisling clapped a hand to her chest.

"Thankfully not. It's just another out of body experience. You're getting good at it though."

Aisling noted the discomfort in her mum's voice. "I'm not going to die, don't worry. I knew what I was doing when I electrocuted myself. I'm getting rather good at that too – first you, now me."

They both gave a nervous chortle.

"Did you lead me here, mum? This must be the fifth plane that Craig – my psychic friend back on earth – was telling me about."

Mum shook her head. "I didn't lead you here, you created a channel that drew me in. I've been residing in the Spirit World, remember?"

Aisling nodded. "The fourth plane. That's the astral world where most souls go after death."

So why had they transcended both the physical plane and the spirit realm? What had Craig said about the fifth dimension? It was where spirits who became masters of their own consciousness went to, and that once they had learned the lessons of their past lives, they could turn into orbs of pure energy.

Aisling felt such a fraud being there among such higher vibrational beings, and in earthly appearance, even if she were a spirit. Shame weighed her down, a heavy, gravitational burden on her soul, pulling her dense spirit towards the silvery ground.

"You have to release your mind, honey. I can feel your energy drawing everything closer with a strong, gravitational pull," said her mum.

It was true; anything near to her began to warp, the hills twisting inwards towards her, the spheres flattening as they floated closer. She was like a magnet of uncertainty.

"Don't be insecure. You have no need to be. You came here for a reason, you just have to figure out why," said her mum.

Aisling studied her mum's face. "How is it you know all this stuff?"

"A decade in the Spirit World has taught me a lot. Though this is my first time here, in this higher plane of existence."

A deep breath cleared her head, even though in reality she wasn't breathing at all, as she had no physical body. That was it; as simple as that. What were the limitations of her form, considering she didn't have a body? If she had no brain, why did she feel any shame? What good did guilt do when she had no head to process such a lower vibrational emotion?

Looking down, she noticed her skin had begun to glow. Her ghostly greyish form had begun to sparkle. What had changed; her thought process?

"This is great, honey, I can feel the power of your self-reflection. Your energy is burning brighter."

Her mum was right. Aisling pressed her lips together, determined to keep up momentum. What next? Craig had said that in order to become a master of one's spirit, you had to connect with the past lives you had led on earth, and understand the lessons you had learned from each life.

Aisling concentrated.

Nope; couldn't remember anything of her past lives. She could have been a carnivorous cave woman or an Egyptian princess, for all she knew. Or maybe she had been nothing at all; maybe this was her first life in physical form.

Yes. Deep down in her core, right where the complex knot of nerve endings fused in her solar plexus, Aisling knew the answer: that she had never been anything in a previous life. She was a blank slate, a new person. In some ways that made life easier; there were fewer lessons to process and evaluate, to see what she had learned.

But she was only nineteen, on the verge of twenty. She hadn't experienced much of life in general. How could she possibly become a master of her own soul?

"You're unburdening yourself of your consciousness, I can feel the energy radiating from you," said her mum.

Weird. How could she unburden a blank slate? Yet, the process of simply thinking about how she had few lessons to learn from must have been a lesson in itself, if she was able to stimulate her consciousness from it.

Wait; what? Her head hurt.

How could it hurt if she had no head?

None of it made any sense.

"You're condensing. Your energy is becoming more concentrated."

I am safe. I am grounded. The mantra played in her head, a relic of a distant yoga class, perhaps. Or was it something that Craig had put in her head? Wherever the words came from, they soothed her.

Then again, how could she be grounded if she had no feet? Not real ones anyway; she was a spiritual imprint, her body in its soul form.

A whooshing sensation made Aisling feel like she were on a rollercoaster. Light emanated from within her core; a cold light spreading its eerie beauty across the strange, silvery landscape.

"You've done it," her mum gasped. "You've turned into an orb."

Aisling tried to speak, but found that she couldn't. Instead of feeling panic, which might have been a natural reaction to learning that she had no mouth, she concentrated her inward thoughts and projected them outwards.

"I've mastered myself. I don't know how I did it, but somehow I did."

"You did it because you realised you know nothing," said a nearby orb, by telepathy.

Aisling was ruffled. She took a moment to process the other orb's answer. Why should she feel anger? It wasn't saying she was stupid; to know nothing probably meant emptiness.

"Emptiness. Yes, I know I'm a blank slate. But I don't know how that taught me enough to master my soul?" Aisling answered through her own telepathic connection.

"Humans only use around ten percent of their brains – and as a species, we have the largest brains per cranium size. Isn't that a waste?" the orb said.

"Ten percent. That's nothing," said Aisling.

"Exactly. The more we learn to fill our brains, the more we realise we don't know anything," the orb continued.

Don't know anything. Nothing. "Only ten percent of Egyptian tombs have been found, they say. There must be so many more Tutankhamuns out there. They haven't even found Nefertiti's tomb yet," Aisling went on.

What had this to do with anything? She was simply repeating information she had heard earlier in the semester during one of her History modules; a throwaway comment.

If ninety percent of her mind was empty space, then what filled that void? After all, nothing was really empty; it was filled with air. That space in the human brain had to be full of matter. Matter, or energy.

"The Egyptians knew so much more than modern humans. Modern humans have dulled their connection with the universe. Fewer and fewer souls are transcending and reaching the higher planes," said the orb.

"And yet I know a being from a higher realm, and she has the power to cause so much harm." Aisling's projected thoughts trailed off, unfinished into the ether.

"If you know of a higher being, then you must be referring to a demigod, or another deity."

"She is. Or at least, she was. She's a fallen goddess and she intends me harm. Not only me, but a man I'm trying to save. He's so much more important than me," said Aisling.

"All souls are equal. None are more important than any others. All that matters is what we learn on the journey."

Energy can neither be created nor destroyed, although it can be converted from one form into another.

Souls are neither more or less important than each other. They can only learn a lifetime's worth and pass on into the next realm.

Everything was cyclical.

But what did moving on into a higher plane of consciousness accomplish? Souls eventually reached the seventh plane. Enlightenment. Nirvana. But if energy was neither created nor destroyed, then it had to all go back into the universe, didn't it?

If Aisling had a head, which she didn't, then it would surely hurt trying to solve such a paradox.

"I wonder can you help me," Aisling began, trying to condense her thoughts.

"You want help with this troublesome demigod, don't you?"

"Yes. I'm emitting so much more energy in this plane of existence than I did before, but it still isn't enough. If I am to defeat her higher energy, I need to bring stronger energy of my own to challenge her."

"You're looking at it all wrong." The orb hovered nearer to Aisling and she sensed its energy pulsating in waves. "She can't be defeated. Only brought back into balance. Good and bad are two sides of the same thing."

Balance. Good and Bad. Yin and Yang. Black and White.

The fifth plane was a place of white light with all its glowing spirit orbs. Cliona radiated a blackness. A frightening dark density; a black hole of despair.

"Will you help me bring balance to her?" Aisling said. She was saying the same thing as before, only phrasing it in a positive light. Is that all it took? Shedding more light on negative aspects; as simple as that?

"Yes. There are a few souls here who wish to transcend one step closer to enlightenment. If we can accomplish the goal of bringing balance to a higher energy sphere, that will draw our energy into the next plane of existence."

Aisling swooped closer to the other orb. Their combined energy radiated brighter, sending a glow across all the crests and troughs, chasing any shadows away.

Chapter twenty-four

There was no noise, only bright light. Bright light and searing pain. Did she even have a body? She must have, as every neurone felt like it were connected to a live electrical wire. It was a cold, shooting pain that emitted in wave after unrelenting wave.

Khaki coloured sky emerged above and three dark silhouettes peered over the edge of the deep pit that she was in, looking up.

Aisling blinked, allowing time for her body to readjust in the Sidhe Realm. She turned her face to the left and looked at Jimbo.

"Aisling, thank goodness you're alive," he gasped.

"Jimbo, you're awake," she said.

"The cold water roused me. There was a strange energy drawing my spirit away from here. I was almost lost."

The water was waist deep. Any longer away and Aisling would have drowned; they both might have. Jimbo's spirit would have entered the fourth plane of spirits and her soul would have been stuck in the Orb Realm.

"I see you're back," Cliona intoned, unable to keep the excitement from her voice. "And just in time for the best part, too."

The water reached Aisling's chest.

"Drowning is one of the kinder ways to go. Aren't you lucky I'm feeling kind today? It's probably the reason why she didn't come when I called. Your fate could have been much worse."

"I don't even know what you're talking about," said Aisling, shaking her head.

"She's talking about the Oilliphéist." Jimbo's tone was sombre.

"You think it'll come at your beck and call, not mine, because you're the descendant of Manannan MacLir, the God of the Sea, don't you?" Cliona spoke in her best schoolmarm voice.

"What's an Oilliphéist?" said Aisling.

Jimbo glared at Cliona. "No, I wouldn't presume to think it would come if I called it. But I *know* it won't come if you try," he said.

"Because you think I'm evil?" Cliona snorted.

"Because your energy isn't strong enough to attract it," said Jimbo matter-of-factly.

Aisling huffed. "I'll assume an Oilliphéist is some kind of sea monster since you're talking about the God of the Sea then, am I right?"

Jimbo's soothing gaze settled on her face and Aisling found her irritation melting away. "It's a creature of legend, so who really knows. Then again, many things I would have thought mere myth have become my reality for the longest possible purgatory of my life in this strange Netherworld, so I wouldn't be surprised if such a beast really did exist."

Aisling held his gaze. While she stared at him, she drew upon her experience in the fifth plane; she had communicated with the other orbs by telepathy. She herself was an orb, a higher spirit: a master. Confidence welled in her like tidal surge. She didn't talk, simply held the connection with Jimbo through their locked eyes.

"Jimbo, I have a plan," said Aisling through her mind.

"Aisling? I can hear your thoughts." Jimbo's mouth didn't open; only his thoughts spoke to her.

"I can deal with Cliona – when the time is right. But I need your help. Can you call the Oilliphéist?"

His brow taughtened, as his thoughts funnelled to her through the channel in their minds. "How would I know if I can when I've never tried?"

"You have to trust me and try. I've brought help from a place I've only just come back from."

His green eyes widened. "You mean, when you were unconscious? Your soul went someplace else?"

She gave one slow, subtle nod. "We'll soon be underwater. That's when I'm going to take action against Cliona. There'll only be one chance. Will you put your trust in me and call the sea monster?"

"Okay, I'll give it a go," Jimbo's thoughts relayed.

Jimbo closed his eyes. No internal thoughts reached her through their telepathic connection; that had to mean he was trying to channel the Oilliphéist. The water in the pit began to churn as the ground shook. Aisling heard a distant rumbling sound. Her body began to sway, buffeted by the waves in their pit. Once or twice, she was swept off her feet and had to tread water as the growing tide reached head height.

Cliona crouched down, leaning between the wafting incense sticks, and dropped the bottom half of an empty eggshell into the pit. It floated on the water surface between Jimbo and herself. Aisling smacked it away; must have been a token of protection that Cliona had issued for herself, though she didn't know what it meant. Cliona was nonplussed at Aisling's reaction; the fallen goddess raised her arms to the skies and uttered an incantation.

In the present, here and now, and fast
I evoke the elemental force at last
I call to the sea and its infinite form
To purify Sidhe and protect us from harm
By taking flesh and eating deep
You may free our spirits, though two you can keep.

Aisling was affronted. "Jimbo and I aren't the ones intending harm – you are. You're the one trying to sacrifice us to a sea monster for your own gain."

Cliona ignored her, repeating the incantation.

The rumbling grew louder and the ground beneath their feet shook. Aisling began to tread water as the ten foot deep pit became full, extinguishing the incense sticks as it flowed over the edges. She turned to Jimbo.

"Call it now, Jimbo. Get it to come and help us – not her." She grabbed his arm, gripping tight. "If there's a chance that you have more power than Cliona to call it, then please – please – save us. Do it now, if you can."

"I'll give it a go, there's no other choice." Jimbo floated on his back, his eyes closed. Aisling moved aside to give him room as he faced the sky, like DaVinci's Vitruvian Man. "Oilliphéist, I summon you now, come for the purpose of Manannan, come to aid the descendant of MacLir, cleanse all malice with your healing waters. Come."

Aisling was impressed; he spoke with an authoritative air that gave weight to his words.

The river was swallowed as a tsunami of black water surged forwards and engulfed the riverbanks, leaving only the isolated crannog. Sidhe were washed out of the forests and swept out of Cliona's palace in the middle of the crannog. The water continued to churn as panicked, flailing Sidhe tried to escape the menacing rumble below them.

Aisling watched, petrified, as white spray fountained high and from its midst a terrible, bony grey head emerged. It looked like a gigantic conger eel, slippery and sleek, except that it had a marine blue bony frill along its back reminiscent of a Spinosaurus. As the colossal beast arched high, she followed the line of its long, grey, muscular form. Its body was as long and wide as a Translink train back in Belfast.

The Oilliphéist opened its bony jaws and dozens of Sidhe, caught by surprise, washed into the black, gaping maw; much like a blue whale eating plankton. Aisling stared in horror, unable to tear her gaze away.

What on earth was she thinking asking Jimbo to call it? She felt sick to the pit of her stomach; it would eat both of them as well as Cliona and all the Sidhe.

Of course, she wasn't on earth at all.

Did that mean the rules were different; did such a sea monster of myth and legend not obey normal biological rules like animals of the deep back on earth? Predators on earth would eat any animal until they'd had enough. Would this beast, this Oilliphéist, really only eat everything except Jimbo and herself?

No blood flowed in the water, and Aisling was thankful that no severed limbs floated either; the Oilliphéist swallowed swathes of Sidhe whole. She couldn't see Jimbo anywhere, nor Cliona either, for that matter. Only endless, black churning water and the roar of waves that pounded in her mind.

"Please, universal energy, reset the balance. Save us from Cliona's wrath, but also, please save us from this diabolical monster. I'm sorry we unleashed it. Please stop this nightmare for us."

Chapter twenty-five

Aisling floated on her back, bobbing on the crests and troughs. Her energy was spent; it was the only way she knew she was still alive as every part of her body ached from swimming. Swimming for what? To save her own life? Not necessary, it seemed. The Oilliphéist had eaten everyone except her. She had been spared. Jimbo too? Who knew; she couldn't see him anywhere. What about Cliona? Couldn't see the Queen of the Banshees either.

The waters receded. Aisling's back bumped against ground and she lay, star-fished on whatever solid surface her body had been washed up on. She calmed herself by staring at the khaki expanse of sky above, until the brightness was imprinted on her retinas. Her nostrils flared and deflated as she sucked air into her lungs to steady her heart. She craned her neck to look downwards along her body and watched the rise and fall of her chest as oxygen flooded her adrenaline-ravaged body. In, out, in and out.

"I am calm. I am grounded. I am centred. I am safe."

Aisling burst into tears. Spit flew from her mouth as she howled. Mucus streamed in rivulets down both cheeks and her tears streamed in torrents, mixing with the snot; tributaries converging to form larger rivers, rivers flowing to the sea. The sea had come to wash away the Sidhe. No more Sidhe, gone with the sea. The Oilliphéist, a physical incarnation of the sea itself, had seen to that.

"Aisling? Where are you?"

She sat bolt upright and wiped her face on her sleeve. "Jimbo? I'm over here."

Jimbo had washed aground a good twenty-or-so feet away from her. He was drenched, his shirt and corduroys clinging to him. Aisling watched as he pushed himself up onto one shaking knee, bracing himself with his elbow on his leg. He sucked strength back into his body through one, massive, inhale and hauled himself up onto two, unsteady feet. Her eyes settled on the outline of his taut chest and abdomen, clear through his clinging shirt and she felt heat rise into her face. Aisling willed her gaze upwards to his eyes, feeling a little guilty. Was she objectifying him if she wanted to peel off his shirt, rather than peel her eyes away from him?

Too hot. She closed her eyes and focused on more breathing to cool herself off.

Jimbo strode across to her and reached for her hands. He held them within his own, warm, strong palms and gave a firm squeeze.

"I was worried you were gone. That – didn't go as I had imagined."

"You have incredible power," she gasped, hearing the awe in her own voice.

"Power I didn't know I wielded," he added, his green eyes wide with innocence.

They held each other's gaze for a few seconds before both were swept into a maelstrom of passion; Aisling breathed the air he exhaled and he, hers as their mouths locked and arms snaked around one another. After a few minutes, within which an infinity of pent-up desire had unleashed, Aisling and Jimbo fell apart.

He licked his lips, tasting her kiss. "As much as I loved that and have wanted to do it since I first set eyes on you, I could have chosen a better moment – we are the last two living creatures in this world now, apart from the Oilliphéist."

Aisling cast her eyes from left to right, sensing the environment, tuning in to the energy of the second plane. "I agree and disagree. Agree, that I have wanted to kiss you too, ever since I had that first taste under the mistletoe when you gave me the tiniest, electrical sting on my lips. And disagree that we aren't the last two living creatures here."

He looked brooding. "Cliona lives, doesn't she? Wait – you're right. We aren't alone."

Aisling watched him revolve on the spot, slow and steady as though sensing an invisible presence. "Are you saying the Oilliphéist is still here?"

"No, it's gone. It did its job. It cleansed the Sidhe. They passed through its energy force and were freed of the negativity and resentment that Cliona had instilled in them under her reign in this Netherworld," said Jimbo.

"But Cliona hasn't changed. I can feel her anger and need for revenge against us. I can feel it like knives, piercing my soul. Her energy is close too – she's nearby. If she gets to them before we get to her, she'll corrupt them again and we'll be back to where we started."

Aisling looked around, wary of the fallen goddess coming to finish what she had started and kill them both. The waters had receded back to the tidal river, leaving only the sacrificial pit still flooded. She stood three feet away from the wooden staves lining its edge; despite the furore with the Oilliphéist, it seemed she had merely floated upwards and not further away, even though she felt as though she had swum a mile.

A surge of hatred behind Aisling made her spin, but a moment too late; Cliona was on top of her. As the Queen of the Banshees toppled forwards, Aisling felt herself falling backwards. With a splash they fell into the deep pool that filled the sacrificial pit.

"Aisling!"

Jimbo's cry was muffled through the water. Blackness engulfed her: it took a moment to realise her eyes were wide open. Aisling felt Cliona's hands on the top of her head and knees on her shoulders; the fallen goddess was going to drown her.

She had to act fast.

Instead of fighting Cliona off, Aisling fumbled in her pocket, her fingers skirting over the bundle of fairy lights. In the darkness, a comforting image came to her, one that empowered her.

Orbs. Higher souls, masters of their consciousness. They had floated to her one by one, their energy touching hers. As they rebounded away, Aisling's own orb had glowed brighter. She carried that higher energy within herself, locked in the ninety percent of her subconscious brain that she hadn't used until recently.

Aisling visualised the healing light in her mind. It glowed in her subconscious, a beacon in the darkness. She visualised the energy of individual orbs floating out of her mind, down her neck, passing through her heart, then along her arm and into the battery case of the fairy lights. The infinite power of the universe travelled through the electrical wires. Each coloured fairy filled up; every bulb flooded with overwhelming healing power.

She wrapped the wire around Cliona's midriff, holding the final bulb against the fallen goddess' heart, and flicked the switch.

Chapter twenty-six

In an instant, the water was gone. The blackness of the sacrificial pit was gone. Cliona was gone. Or was she; her energy was still present?

Aisling had become an orb again, as though her body had spontaneously burst into pure energy. Did that mean she had electrocuted herself along with Cliona, maybe even killed herself for real this time, considering that the fairy lights had been supercharged with energy from the fifth plane of existence?

Fear set in. She hadn't intended to kill herself; certainly not when she hadn't finished what she needed to do. How would an orb consigned to the fifth plane rebalance the negative energy of a fallen goddess from a higher plane? It was too great an undertaking, especially alone.

Jimbo, I need you. Aisling concentrated her thoughts; could her higher telepathic connection as a master of the soul connect with Jimbo's subconscious self?

Her own subconsciousness answered: no. No, they couldn't connect. Not because Jimbo didn't have a finely tuned spiritual awareness of his own, but because he had already done his job. His role had been to call the Oilliphéist to cleanse the Sidhe, which he had done. Now, it was up to her to play her part in rebalancing Cliona.

No time for fear; she had a mission. If she couldn't undertake such a task alone, then why had she even become a master of her soul in the first place?

Fear. She could see it, lingering like a dark swarm of angry, buzzing insects before her. The miniscule, buzzing insects condensed into a dark form; at first it was an irregular mass, but gradually began to take shape. Two legs. Two arms. A dome on top, like a head.

There was no mistaking that the psychic insects had taken Cliona's form. Her outline, a silhouette of lower lifeforms, hovered before Aisling, and she was seized with fear.

"Fear is a useless emotion. It only serves to hold me back," said Aisling, with her mind.

Insect-form Cliona didn't move, only wavered as the buzzing creatures spread out then regrouped.

"I lived most of my childhood and nearly all of my teens in fear that I would die. Die like my mum did. But I'm sick of living in fear. I won't be a slave to fear. And I certainly won't be a slave to my fear of you," she willed her mind.

The angry swarm of psychic insects burst, each tiny dot flying outwards: a supernova on the blank fabric of the universe. A pixelated image on the television screen of her mind.

Fear was gone. In place of it was a colour: Aisling radiated a new hue. Gone was the greyish white orb. Her spirit colour was now pink, like the sky before a thunderstorm.

Why was she changing colour? Surely white energy was the purest form; the most enlightened energy in the universe? If she had already been a glowing white orb, then why did she now radiate pink light?

She must have done something wrong. Had she lowered her energy, her vibrational frequency? Was she no longer a master of her soul because she had changed from a greyish white glowing sphere to a concentrated pink aura?

Panic began to set in. Self-fuelled paranoia had taken root in her consciousness. It wriggled as the seed of self-doubt implanted deep.

Aisling forced her logical side to overtake her emotional one, proactive thoughts usurping the irrational feelings flooding the vacuum of her consciousness. What plane came after the fifth one, or orbs? Craig said it was the sixth plane; a rainbow spectrum where consciousness was stripped into its primary colours. Stripped bare. That had to be what was happening to her soul: it was being dissolved into its compound elements.

Fear and now paranoia. She had conquered fear and now she was tackling paranoia. How straightforward it was; she had to conquer each negative emotion as it was presented in its simplest form.

Metaphorical deep breath. After all, she had become an orb, without a body; consciousness floating free.

Was there a dark shadow beginning to form to her left, or was she imagining it?

Yes, a dark entity. Harmful energy pulsated from it. *The sixth plane is the last place where evil can reside*. Craig's words, now revolving in the sphere of her consciousness, like a protective barrier.

Did the dark entity mean her harm, or was it merely a manifestation of the paranoia she hoped to rid herself of? Aisling concentrated on it. As before with the swarm of psychic insects, the shadow form resembled Cliona. Could she ever escape the fallen goddess, and her hatred for humankind; indeed, her fury towards the third plane of existence on earth in its entirety.

Aisling searched deep in the pool of her consciousness for the right answer. "We haven't stolen the earth from you, our ancestors earned the right to take your place in the third plane of existence. The Sidhe were defeated. Your people went underground into the fairy mounds. It shouldn't be about revenge. We all live – and evolve – on a spectrum of universal energy. If you can't learn and grow, then that's your own undoing and nobody else's."

The dark shadow began to dissipate. Like a cloud, diffusing into the fabric of its surroundings, the shadow faded into the ether.

Paranoia had been overcome.

And in its place? By rights she should have been angry at Cliona, not paranoid about the Queen of the Banshees' wrath. Aisling wasn't angry though. There she was, stuck in the rainbow realm, the sixth plane of existence. Cliona was there too, though so far in a couple of different forms: clustered fear and shadowy paranoia. Did that mean she was creating Cliona and that if it weren't for her feelings towards the fallen goddess, Cliona wouldn't exist in this plane at all? But, that couldn't be true; Cliona had once resided in the sixth plane before corruption had made her descend to lower existences.

Maybe she had more power than Cliona here in this realm, especially since Cliona had fallen from grace here, yet she remained untainted in the sixth plane.

Aisling swelled, her sphere expanding, like a flower unfurling its petals. She had more power than Cliona, it was true. Cliona assumed the form of whatever she, Aisling, chose her to be. Cliona was nothing without her; only a mere manifestation of whatever Aisling allowed her to be.

But, was that a good thing?

Pride. It made sense; the next emotion she had to confront was her ego.

There she was, on cue, just as she crept into Aisling's thoughts. A hazy, grainy Cliona began to form as though made out of grains of sand swept into a desert storm.

Being egotistical defied what she believed; that universal energy was distributed evenly among every life force in existence. No; feeling herself superior to other beings, however imbalanced their own positive and negative energy fields were, was nothing to be proud of.

The sand-grain Cliona exploded into a billion miniscule particles and was gone.

Aisling's orb resumed its normal size, no longer swollen and bloated with pride. There was nothing to feel a sense of accomplishment about in feeling superior to Cliona. Pride had been overcome; Aisling glowed blue. Blue, as serenity swept over her. Blue, and calm, from the innermost depths of her spirit radiating outwards. Blue, next on the spectrum of the rainbow of her soul.

She could afford to take a moment to be one with the feelings washing over her on this journey. Hadn't she come so far, tackling her own, personal emotional hurdles: her own seven deadly sins? How many had she overcome? Fear, paranoia, pride. Halfway through the rainbow spectrum of consciousness and somewhat centred. Yes, she could afford to take pause.

What would it take to leave the sixth plane? Could a soul exit such a realm, their journey unfinished? Aisling wracked her consciousness to see if she could find another way out. Hypothetically speaking, of course, but surely there had to be a 'cheat sheet' for souls to leave unencumbered?

Oh dear; she had activated a new sensation. Her orb began to vibrate this time, buzzing like a phone trying to relay an incoming call. Only, what incoming call was she trying to relay to herself?

It was all so much bother. If she had a body, she would have been tired from the effort. What was the point in all of it anyway? She was stuck in a vacuous realm of nonexistence and for all she knew, would be there, floating forever.

Buzzing forever. Vibrating and buzzing into a vacuum from which she'd never return. Unable, unwilling. Lost to herself, lost to all she knew. Far removed from Cliona too, the foe she was supposed to tackle.

Tackle, how? Who knew, who cared? All that mattered was how the blue light emanating from her felt self-soothing. Why move on in the spectrum when it felt so good right there, where she was?

Procrastination. If she could have sighed, she would have, except she had no mouth. Indecision, maybe even denial. Sloth, according to the seven deadly sins.

Procrastination-Cliona began to take shape as a smoky form, a sinister form that was opaque, yet transparent, formless, yet fixed in shape. How could that be the case? It was as though this Cliona couldn't make up its mind how it wanted to appear; or rather, Aisling's own consciousness couldn't decide what it wanted to do.

"I have to move on from this. As comfortable as it is, in the here and now, it won't last. Good becomes bad, and bad becomes good. Life changes, moves on and takes new forms. It's all part of the cycle," said her consciousness into the vast expanse of the sixth plane.

In the here and now. Aisling had heard those words before. They had been spoken by Cliona, when the fallen goddess had tried in vain to summon the Oilliphéist. Why was she repeating Cliona's words, even as assurance to herself? Did that mean her consciousness was starting to meld with Cliona's? Was that part of a greater universal test she had to endure – and pass?

So be it. If binding her consciousness to that of Cliona's imbalanced soul was her task, she would do it.

The smoky, Sloth-Cliona dissipated into the ether, absorbed into nothingness, at one with the vast, empty rainbow realm. Aisling's blue light shone green.

How easy for Cliona, though. Aisling watched the spot where the smoky fallen goddess had disappeared. The Queen of the Banshees could come and go as she pleased, and so easily too. Free floating, free forming, in and out of the ether with not a care. How easy for her.

Aisling seethed. Not so easy for herself, on the other hand. Yes, she had conquered fear, paranoia, pride and now procrastination – but it was slow progress. She was green. Green with jealousy. The green-eyed monster hated Cliona for the goddess still had the upper hand, even when she was fallen, even when she didn't belong.

Envy. How simple, how fast she had recognised the emotion and owned responsibility for it.

The Cliona that formed before her looked pristine, like an ice sculpture. It glistened with a smooth, immaculate beauty; one that Aisling couldn't compare to, no matter how hard she tried.

"You can glide in and out of this rainbow realm, this sixth plane of existence but you choose to abuse that ability. If I could become that level of immortal soul, I would cherish it, treasure it for what it was worth," Aisling channelled from the depths of her subconscious self.

But what was the act of cherishing and treasuring something, if one hadn't abused such power in the first place? To have no basis of comparison gave no sense of weight to that kind of accomplishment; it was inherently of no value without having been through a tarnished act, in order to give it value.

Tarnished. A goddess who had fallen and become Queen of the Banshees. Tarnished. An eight year old girl full of innocence who had electrocuted her own mother.

If Aisling had a mouth she would have gasped. Who was she to envy Cliona, when she was in the same position? Tarnished. What would it take to polish a stain on a tarnished soul?

Pristine Cliona began to melt, its perfect face melting, its unblemished façade running, showing the imperfections underneath. They appeared as nodules in the ice-sculpture figure standing before Aisling.

Not so perfect after all, and nothing to envy. They were equal souls in the universal scales of balance.

Just as the bubbling puddle of what remained of Cliona disappeared into nothingness, Aisling emitted a radiant new light. Envy had been overcome and now she shone yellow.

Five colours of the rainbow: Violet; indigo; blue; green and now yellow. Aisling was dispersing into her primary compounds, the essential components of what made her a whole being.

Equal. She was equal to Cliona. In terms of their universal energy, had they been rebalanced? Not so, if the colour spectrum had anything to do with it. What was left to overcome? Two colours, before true white, pure energy. Orange and red, the last two colours of the rainbow.

What would happen once she had accomplished the last two challenges of her soul, revealing her true self? If she was equal with Cliona now, did that mean the former goddess would be vanquished?

A worm of an idea began to burrow upwards through the detritus of her subconscious. Aisling tried to suppress it, but Craig's words stuck in her mind, holding her back:

The sixth plane is the last place where evil can reside.

Maybe, if she were honest, she didn't want to be equal with Cliona. When she had felt below Cliona, she had envied her. Now that they were on an equal footing, she wanted more. She had to admit it to herself – it was better to be honest–

She wanted to take over Cliona's place in the rainbow realm. She wanted to be superior to the goddess.

Once more, her orb began to expand, a star becoming a supernova.

"But I've recognised the challenge, haven't I? Is honesty not the first step to self-improvement?" her orb beseeched the universe.

She was becoming bigger, and hotter. The sphere of self burned like a furnace.

Just as she grew in size, a fiery, burning Cliona materialised before her, mirroring the intensity of her orb. The flame-Cliona burned with a yellow-orange intensity, tongues of fire licking upwards into the vast unknown of the rainbow realm.

"Greed, yes. I'm greedy. I want to take over you, Cliona, and assume your place in the sixth realm."

The supernova of Aisling's soul grew large and orange. Cliona, in response, burned with hot, orange fire.

"I don't actually think I can stop this feeling. I'm not sure I can overcome this challenge. It's too self-fulfilling – I think."

Fire-Cliona and Supergiant star-Aisling began to merge, sphere and flame crossing into one another's energy fields. Aisling couldn't say at what point Cliona disappeared among the fire ball of flame and the burning inferno of her own energy, but the fallen goddess disappeared, this time unlike the other times.

Each other time, Cliona's form, whether shadow, or pixelated dots, or an insect swarm, or smoke, or ice; each form vanished in front of Aisling in a manner that was clear to see and discernible from her own orb form. This time was different. Aisling couldn't tell where she ended and Cliona began.

Had her gluttony consumed Cliona? Had the challenge of her soul backfired; instead of overcoming her greed, her personal sixth deadly sin of gluttony, it had consumed herself and Cliona in the process?

All she knew was that she now glowed orange. A bright, burning, orange ball of fire like a Red Supergiant. Whatever happened now was beyond her control; her energy was taking her down a self-fulfilling path that would end in with her soul imploding, completely.

Her orb continued to burn with the power of its own fuel, a raging inferno. Yes, with the power of whatever wrath had been unleashed from the depths of her subconscious, she would consume every last part of Cliona's persona, until the Queen of the Banshees no longer existed.

Wrath. The Red Supergiant of Aisling's star continued to expand, violently ejecting energy into the vacuous rainbow realm. She was a timebomb, waiting to implode.

Wrath. Aisling reached the final colour on the spectrum of her soul: red. She would consume every part of Cliona. That was how she would bring balance to the former goddess; by wiping her out.

With a dramatic boom, the orb of Aisling's consciousness exploded outwards then collapsed inwards. Everything that she had ever been, and was until mere nanoseconds before, had gone.

Chapter twenty-seven

Aisling opened her eyes. She closed them again, then reopened them to make sure. Yes, she was certain, she had eyes. That meant she was back in physical form.

But where? On earth? In the Sidhe Realm? If she really was in physical form, was she herself or had she been born again?

She reached for her face. Her warm fingers scuttled over her cheeks, across her closed eyelids and over her clammy forehead.

Warm lips brushed hers. Air blew into her mouth. Light fingertips tapped one cheek and then the other. "Aisling, are you awake? Thank heavens you're alive."

Jimbo's voice. Aisling opened her eyes, but could only see white. "Where are you? I can hear you, but I don't see you? Where am I?"

"You're with me, and thank goodness you're alive," said Jimbo's voice, close to her right ear.

Aisling sat up. "Why can't I see anything?"

"I think you were unconscious for the longest time. You were underwater with Cliona for the longest time – at least fifteen minutes."

Fifteen minutes. More than enough time for a person to drown. More than enough time for a person to leave one plane of existence and transcend in another.

"I was gone. I went to another dimension."

"I know," said Jimbo, his voice sad. "After I saw you both writhing in that pit, I jumped in to rescue you. But I couldn't find you – only the wooden sides – and it was too black to see anything. Where did you go?"

"A place where souls get stripped down into their most basic energy forms. A rainbow realm."

"Did Cliona go with you?" Jimbo's voice was hopeful.

Aisling nodded. "I think I might have consumed her there – with my anger."

"Anger? But you don't have any. Cliona was the one who wanted vengeance against us."

Aisling turned in the direction of his voice, but could still only see brightness. "I know I'm not angry. I can't explain it either. An unconscious, buried part of my mind wanted to obliterate Cliona and take her place in that dimension – the sixth plane of existence. It's too hard to explain."

"Try me. I'm listening." Jimbo took her hands in his.

She took a deep breath, grateful to be able to have lungs that could fill with air. "It was like, my soul went through seven stages of letting go of negative feelings that were buried inside me. Fear, paranoia, pride, procrastination, envy, greed and rage. One by one, my soul changed colour as I was able to conquer those demons. All except for the last two – greed and rage. I couldn't overcome my gluttony and wrath. They consumed everything – both me and Cliona. I think I failed."

"No, you didn't." Jimbo stroked her cheek. "You and I both succeeded in what we had to do. I called the Oilliphéist, which came and cleansed the Sidhe. You reset Cliona's energy and you became a higher soul yourself."

A hazy outline of Jimbo began to appear and Aisling concentrated on his silhouette, allowing her physical self to readjust to being in the second plane of existence. After such a soul-enlightening experience in the sixth plane, it would take time for her earthly body to acclimatise.

"I didn't reset Cliona's energy though, I wiped her out," said Aisling, with a profound sadness that surprised her. I guess I didn't know the power of my own energy."

"You didn't wipe her out, I can feel her life force," said Jimbo.

Aisling focused on his eyes. She could see the mellow, soothing colour of his lime-green eyes, thankful that her body had almost completely restored its senses. She focused on his blonde hair, rippling as a gentle wind lifted the strands off his head. She let her eyes settle on his soft lips, the corners upturned in a placid smile. She saw Jimbo, but she wasn't looking at him.

She was sensing everything around her. The wet grass below where she sat. The khaki-brown sky above.

Aisling was in tune with her environment, every neurone alert, every sense acute.

"You're right," she said. "Cliona's essence is in this realm. But her energy has changed and I can't tell from where it's coming. I don't see the source."

Wavy lines distorted the horizon when Aisling focused on points at a distance. At first, she thought they were heat waves, but when she turned back to Jimbo, the wavy lines distorted him too, though only when she trained her gaze on one distinct spot.

What was going on?

"Aisling, what is it? You look troubled?"

She shook her head. "It's okay. I'm just trying to figure out what these strange, wavy lines I'm seeing are. You know, I think they might actually be Cliona's life force. The strange thing is, though, I'm seeing them as an energy force around me and they're affecting things that I see – both up close and far away."

She reached for Jimbo, and the wavy lines parted around her hand and arm, like ripples of water disturbed by a stone being thrown into a pond. Aisling tried to touch the wavy lines and they danced around her hand, flowing in the gaps between her fingers.

"Cliona's energy is coming from me. If I ever needed any proof that I've consumed her, then this is it," she said.

"Consumed isn't the right word though, as she isn't gone," Jimbo added.

"So, you can see the wavy lines – her energy – too?"

"No. But I can sense it, just as I can sense the Sidhe. They're coming closer."

He was right. Aisling jumped to her feet as a couple of fairy folk became a dozen, then a crowd, then a wall of figures surrounding them both. As they approached, she sensed only benign energy from them, no hostility. Jimbo was right; their energy had been reset by the Oilliphéist.

"You came back to us, from the place of higher knowledge," said one of the Sidhe. Aisling recognised one of the guards who had flanked Cliona on her right side, while she had overlooked the sacrificial pit.

"You," said another, in an awed voice. "You're a vision."

"Yes," said a third. "A dream."

Dream. Vision. Aisling. Not Cliona, Aisling.

"That's right, the meaning of my name – Aisling – is a dream, or a vision."

"The name was chosen for you before you were born," said another Sidhe; Aisling recognised the other guard who had flanked Cliona on her left side.

"I know. My mum picked it," she said.

"No, the spirits in the place of higher knowledge picked it. It was predestined, but always a part of who you are," said one of the Sidhe.

"Who I am?" said Aisling. "I'm still me, I've just been – stripped to my base consciousness."

"You haven't. You're simply whole again," said another Sidhe.

"Whole again? I don't understand. Was I damaged before?" said Aisling.

"Your spirit was incomplete. Yours and Cliona's. Your fates were always intertwined."

Aisling digested the last speaker's words. *Your fates were always intertwined.*

"Are you saying, Aisling and Cliona were related to each other?" Jimbo's green eyes were puzzled.

"Aisling was always Cliona – and Cliona was always Aisling. At least, in spirit," answered another Sidhe.

Aisling thought of all the supernatural experiences that she'd had recently. *Recently.* "If my spirit was really an incomplete part of Cliona's, and our two spirits were actually torn halves that needed to be re-joined, then why did I not sense any of this from the moment I was born?"

She didn't need to wait for an answer; she already knew. Her soul needed to be at the right stage, a receptive state, to accept the universal truth: that it was a small part of a larger spiritual entity. One that had been incomplete and floating, lost in the ether, for many thousands of years.

Chapter twenty-eight

Orange and red streaks of light radiated out of the crown of her head into the far reaches of the black expanse. Above, the stars twinkled with their cold, distant glow. They couldn't help, wouldn't intervene. Why should they? It had happened to her alone. One soul, falling far.

Cliona tumbled; or at least the sensation of falling overwhelmed what few senses she had left. Where was she destined? One of the lower planes of existence; but which one?

She landed with a bump. Wherever she had arrived, she was grounded, and safe.

Cliona stood up. Long, silvery hair blew around her face. When she swiped it back, it dangled to her waist. She had a form again, the first time in many hundreds of thousands of years. The fact that she had a body – a human, female body – meant only one thing. She was on earth. The third plane of existence.

She took a moment to explore herself. She had four fingers and an opposable thumb, further proof that she was a human being. She let her fingers slide into the hollows of her cheeks and eye sockets and from there spread outwards, fanning across her domed forehead, scuttling down over her pointed chin. The last time she had been on earth her forehead had been shorter and had receded into a low-lying hairline, same as her kin. She had been able to think and talk, to worship the gods of nature and feel love, and her soul had been able to flourish with the challenges of living in a cold, hostile environment where her people wore furs to keep warm. She had been elevated in that lifetime to a shaman of her people, and beyond death of the flesh, her soul had continued its journey towards enlightenment. The sixth plane of existence. She had become more than a master of her soul; an immortal. A goddess. So close to enlightenment, but so far.

So far. Here she was, set to journey once again through the physical plane. This time, with a broken soul. Splintered.

But what was missing? She still felt like herself. Nothing felt incomplete.

Wait a minute; what about the orange and red light that had radiated out of her fallen soul. Two colours? What part of her personality did they represent? Where had they gone?

***

The vast, stygian expanse gave her a sense of agoraphobia. It was like floating on a sea without ever seeing a horizon; no hope of washing ashore anywhere, ever.

She felt even more lonesome after watching the kaleidoscope of light that had peeled away from her and dropped below. Five colours: violet, indigo, blue, green and yellow light had gradually dimmed as the cluster of twinkling lights had tumbled towards the blue and green sphere below. Earth. If part of her that had been torn away was falling towards the physical plane for another journey, then what of the rest of her? She floated onwards, emitting a soft reddish-orange glow, as she let the universe embrace her.

All she could do now was watch, with envy, as the five rainbow streaks swirled ever further below and manifested into a vestige of a soul. A soul that wreaked havoc on the inhabitants below. A soul born into the world full of malice, and vengeance against humankind and jealousy for all they accomplished. A soul swept into an underworld, where it set up dominance and established a kingdom among the fairy folk.

Yes, she had split. Her soul was incomplete. If the larger half below was full of anger and hatred for humanity, then what of the two fragments of the personality that floated, lost in space? Why couldn't they too have a life; albeit an incomplete one?

Many thousands of years had passed on earth while she had drifted in the endless void of space. Yes, it was now her turn to return to the physical plane and learn, once more, in the journey of life. A journey that would hopefully allow her fractured soul to heal itself once more.

***

Aisling jumped, as the last piece of the jigsaw puzzle floated from her unconscious mind and embedded in her frontal cortex. She knew who she was; and this time, she would remember forever.

She looked at each of the Sidhe in turn. Each and every living being that stood before her, a loyal follower in the second plane of existence, had lived alongside the living larger part of her soul in the Sidhe Realm since the first humans had overtaken Ireland. Aisling knew how long that had been, not with Cliona's memories, but her own. She was a whole, complete spirit now: Cliona and Aisling combined. They had resided there for nearly 10,000 years, after the ice had receded, allowing settlers to arrive from the European continent by boat.

"I'm human now, in this lifetime, but I'm also Sidhe. Being fairy – and human – makes me stronger. I am a child of both the second plane and third plane of existence – both the Sidhe Realm and on earth." Aisling pinched the skin on her hand. "I'm born in a flesh and blood body that belongs in the physical realm, but I have an immortal soul."

"Are you saying that you're leaving us?" said one of the many faces in the crowd.

"I have to return to my world. I have flesh and blood family there – family who are descended from the ancestors, the first Milesians who watched us descend into these fairy mounds for the very first time."

"Aisling made many wrongs right," said Jimbo. He stood on her right side and slipped his fingers between hers, their hands linked. "She saved me from the wrongful wrath of the dominant, damaged part of her soul. She showed me that I am alive, that my life isn't yet over. But neither is hers — nor yours. The Oilliphéist cleansed all of your souls, so that you may live a life unburdened in this beautiful, pristine realm."

"Yes, we understand all that. We are more fortunate than those of you in the third plane, an earth that is now on the cusp of a climate change that will also wipe clean its inhabitants, as we have been wiped clean. We are fortunate too to have leaders in you both — the descendant of the sea god himself, Manannan MacLir, and Clionaisling — our dream and vision that we foresaw returning to us, goddess of love and beauty, Queen of the Banshees of the Tuatha Dé Danaan."

"Clionaisling," she mouthed. "I could get used to that."

Clionaisling and Jimbo turned to one another and smiled. Jimbo squeezed her interlaced fingers and she squeezed his back.

Chapter twenty-nine

Clionaisling and Jimbo stood on the riverbank, not far from the lair where Jimbo had hidden from Cliona and the Sidhe for over a hundred years. This was the starting point where Aisling had begun her journey in the Sidhe Realm; and it would be the starting point to return to Belfast. She took the dowsing rods that were handed to her, recovered from the riverbank where she had dropped them. The holly and hawthorn sprigs were still attached to the copper tubes. Clionaisling placed the one with holly in her right hand and placed the rod with hawthorn in Jimbo's left hand.

"Are you ready to go back?" she said.

Jimbo took a deep breath, his chest swelling, and exhaled. "I don't know why I'm nervous, but yes. Yes, I'm ready."

"It makes complete sense that you'd be nervous. You haven't been on earth for a really long time – longer than a normal lifetime."

"Then again, I'm not normal," he said with a half-smile.

The corners of her own mouth twitched upwards. "Neither am I."

"Here's to being abnormal together," said Jimbo.

They touched the ends of their dowsing rods together. With her left hand holding the dowsing rod, Clionaisling reached into her back pocket and found there the battery case of her trusty fairy lights. Now battered and weather-worn, ordinarily they wouldn't have worked either. But like Jimbo and Clionaisling, they were abnormal too. Energy from the fifth plane of existence, the Orb Realm, resided in them; along with Clionaisling's own lifeforce, bottled like a genie in a lamp. She flicked the switch and the reaction was immediate; the roundhouse and all its inhabitants disappeared as a blanket of white light cloaked both herself and Jimbo.

"What happens now?" said Jimbo.

"We follow the dowsing rods back to our home," she said.

Clionaisling took the first step into the brightness. Jimbo copied her, walking alongside, with the dowsing rods touching. They walked, blind in the light, their feet moving for an indeterminate amount of passing time.

"We aren't going anywhere. Our feet are moving on the spot, but we're going nowhere," said Jimbo, a note of despair in his voice.

"Don't be deceived. It felt like this when I passed through from earth to here in the first place. We should get some signals soon to show us we're on the right path."

"Aisling, honey, you're going the right way," said her mum's voice.

"Mum, I can hear you." Clionaisling gave Jimbo a reassuring smile. "It's my mum. She's my spirit guide."

"I can sense you now, darling, because you're closer to the third plane," said her mum.

"Are you back in the Spirit Realm?"

"Yes, I'm in the Plane of Light, the fourth plane of existence. You're passing between realms now, moving closer to the physical one."

A clacking noise sounded close to Clionaisling's left ear; the constant sound like a metronome. "The ball bearings, I can hear them."

"Aisling?" said Liv's voice, disembodied in the ether. "Oh my God, Aisling, I swear I heard you just now, it's giving me goosebumps."

Liv's voice faded behind them with a faint echo. Clionaisling had a vision of Liv, imprinted in her mind, as Liv sat in the front garden of her house back in Stranmillis.

"We just moved through my house – our house – didn't we?" said Jimbo.

Excitement welled in the pit of Clionaisling's stomach. "Yes. You felt it too."

They kept marching. Her mum's voice drifted to the left of them and then flitted to the right, offering words of encouragement on their journey.

"Keep going honey. You're nearly there. Just a little longer and you'll be home. Follow the flame – Craig is moving with you in the real world, he'll guide you."

A flash of yellow light materialised before them as they walked. It disappeared from view fast as it had arrived, like a will o' the wisp.

"I see it. I see your candle light, Craig," Clionaisling gasped.

Craig didn't respond. Maybe his connection wasn't as strong, since he was moving too fast.

"I see something else. It looks like a dome." Jimbo pointed ahead. "I've seen that thing – you had it in your house."

The golf umbrella. Clionaisling trained her gaze on it as they approached. Hundreds of coloured lights twinkled behind it: the Christmas tree in Uncle Gerry's house. "Eoin, I'm coming. Thank you for holding my brolly so that I could find my way."

"Aisling? Are you here?" echoed Eoin's voice, as though through a tunnel.

"Yes, I'm here." Clionaisling forgot herself for a moment, waving her hand with the dowsing rod in the hope of attracting Eoin's attention. With the connection broken; the white light faded. At first she saw grey, then a swirl of merging colours. Clionaisling let her dazzled eyes acclimatise to the change. She was standing in the open doorway of Uncle Gerry's living room, with Jimbo in the hallway behind her right shoulder, his own dowsing rod dangling at his left hip.

Eoin stood with the golf umbrella touching the Christmas tree as she had instructed him. He lowered it and rubbed his tired biceps with a sigh. "That was a workout. I held it up for an hour, but I don't think I could've done so for much longer. But you made it, you're here."

He set the brolly down and crossed the room to her. Clionaisling pulled him into a tight bear hug that brought a blush to his face. He patted her upper back in response, then pulled away and looked at her, his eyes magnified through his thick glasses.

"Yes, I made it and I brought company." Clionaisling gestured to Jimbo then Eoin in turn. "Jimbo, meet my friend, Eoin. Eoin, this is Jimbo, the mysterious ghost who lived in my house."

Eoin turned his magnified eyes to Jimbo. His warm smile faded, as did the blush in his cheeks. He cleared his throat then let a polite smile return to his face instead as he offered a hand. "A ghost in the flesh. Nice to meet you. I've heard so much about you."

"Pleased to make your acquaintance. A friend of Clionaisling's is a friend of mine," said Jimbo.

"Clionaisling?" said Eoin, turning to her.

"Long story," she said, with a short laugh.

"Can't wait to hear all about it. The others have just arrived – I'm guessing they'll want to hear all about it too."

Chapter thirty

"Wow, Aisling, why didn't you say that Jimbo was such a dish?"

Liv gawped with her jaw hanging open and Clionaisling felt heat rise in the back of her neck and ears, creeping across into her face. Jimbo kept a polite smile on his face, his expression betraying nothing about how he felt. He was from a different age, one where she was sure girls didn't brazenly, shamelessly, flirt with men. Still, she couldn't blame Liv. Jimbo really was that attractive. Clionaisling couldn't help a boastful smile at her friend, as her chest swelled.

"Youse lot are the best friends. You really believed me, and came through for me, when I needed you most." Clionaisling smiled at them in turn; Liv and

Eoin on the sofa, Craig on the recliner, and Jimbo in the other armchair next to her.

"I have a feeling your name is no longer Aisling. I sense a change in your aura." Craig turned to her. "Am I right?"

She nodded. "I go by the name of Clionaisling now."

"Hmm. Cliona and Aisling. Interesting. I need to hear how your energy merged," said Craig. "And how you made it back safely – with your new friend, Jim Murphy, no less."

Clionaisling reached for Jimbo's hand and gave it a reassuring squeeze, then turned to Craig. "Did you see me vanish, when we were at Friar's Bush – or disappear into the trunk of the Maytree? That's what I saw happen to Jimbo when he got taken into the Sidhe Realm."

Craig shook his head. "I saw you go around behind the Maytree as you picked the mushrooms from the fairy ring and ate them one by one. I admit, I had my eyes closed as I meditated while you did that, to help you pass across the planes of existence, you see. When I opened my eyes and checked, you were gone. I searched among the brambles, but there was no sign of you anywhere. It was as though you'd disappeared into thin air."

Clionaisling took a deep breath and stared at the twinkling lights of the Christmas tree to gather her thoughts. "I don't know where to begin. It's such a long story."

Jimbo slipped his hand over hers and stroked the top with his thumb. "Let me try. You can fill in any gaps."

Clionaisling listened as Jimbo summarised her journey into the Sidhe Realm: how Cliona had planned to sacrifice them by drowning, and how they had worked as a team to cleanse the Sidhe by summoning the Oilliphéist and rebalance Cliona's vengeful nature. He even explained her journey into the sixth plane and how her incomplete soul had reattached to Cliona's in such detail that she couldn't have done a better job herself. He finished with their journey back to the physical realm by using the dowsing rods. From time to time, Craig, Eoin and Liv glanced at her with awed smiles. Clionaisling averted her eyes from all the attention and looked back to the comforting lights of the Christmas tree, letting them calm her spirit.

"There was a moment when I could have sworn I smelled your perfume passing me by. I was sitting in your garden, with my back to the holly bush like you'd told me, and there it was, drifting near my nose as close as someone walking by on the street." Liv's eyes were wide and glassy. "I knew you'd seen my signal – the Newton's Cradle – so I wasn't worried that you had got lost, so I jumped up and dashed out onto the street. That's when I saw two dark shadows."

"Dark shadows?" Clionaisling thought of how Jimbo had first appeared to her, as a black, shadowy form. "I know how that works now. Our physical bodies were in a different plane of existence, so here on earth, we looked like ghosts."

"It was so spooky, especially under the lamppost light – two dark, shifty forms," said Liv, still looking spooked. "I messaged Eoin to let him know you were on your way and then I made my own way here."

"Did you see us materialise here, in the living room?" said Clionaisling to Eoin.

Eoin shook his head. "There was a gust of cold air, as though the front door had opened, though I hadn't heard it unlock. I saw you just standing there in the doorway, with Jimbo behind you in the hall."

"Well, anyway, we're back." Back in the real world, though something was missing; not her mum's presence, as Clionaisling knew her spirit guide had gone back to the fourth plane, after leading her home. "Where's Uncle Gerry? Is he here?"

As though on cue, Uncle Gerry's squat, bulky frame appeared in the doorway. His eyes were narrowed under his thick grey eyebrows and his silver moustache bristled. "Aisling, princess, what are you doing here? This is an unexpected visit."

"I know, I'm sorry. I hope it isn't a bad time. It's rather long to explain. Did Eoin have a chance to tell you?"

Uncle Gerry's frown deepened. "Who?"

Clionaisling gestured to Eoin, and he gave a small wave from the sofa by the Christmas tree.

Uncle Gerry looked behind Eoin at the Christmas tree and his eyes grew round and fearful. "You should've told me you were coming – I would've taken down the tree."

Clionaisling felt Uncle Gerry's strong hands under her armpits, raising her out of her chair, his bear-like bulk blocking her view of the Christmas tree. He ushered her into the kitchen, with a protective grasp on both of her shoulders.

"Uncle Gerry, you're misunderstanding. The Christmas tree isn't a problem for me anymore – and it never will be again."

Clionaisling stood with her back against the kitchen sink, still grasping the downsing rod with holly attached. Uncle Gerry blocked her exit out of the kitchen. Jimbo appeared behind Uncle Gerry in the doorway. His six foot frame towered over Uncle Gerry and his handsome face was crumpled with annoyance.

"What's the problem here?" said Jimbo.

Clionaisling appreciated Jimbo's intervention; it was probably his Edwardian sense of protecting a lady's honour that had made him come to her aid. It might have looked like Uncle Gerry was manhandling her. Clionaisling softened her gaze as she looked at him, then hardened it as she turned back to Uncle Gerry.

Uncle Gerry moved aside to let Jimbo into the kitchen. Jimbo stood between them, though not blocking Clionaisling's view of Uncle Gerry.

"Do I know you?" Uncle Gerry narrowed his eyes. "You look so familiar. I swear I've seen your face before. Have we met?"

"You might know him," said Clionaisling. "He used to live in my house – Granda's place in Stranmillis."

"You were a tenant? I don't remember dad ever letting the place out to you," said Uncle Gerry.

Clionaisling flashed a secret smile to Jimbo, who returned it. "He wasn't a tenant. He wouldn't have looked like this either. More of a dark shadow, really."

Uncle Gerry continued to look at Jimbo, not Clionaisling. "Aren't you a busker? I swear I've seen a fella in town who looks the spitting image of you. He plays a fiddle sometimes at Corn Market."

Jimbo guffawed. "I have no musical talents at all. You must be thinking of someone else."

"Jimbo's so good-looking, he's got one of those faces that everyone thinks they know. Kind of like the handsome next door neighbour that everyone wants to have," said Clionaisling.

"Are you two together?" Uncle Gerry's eyes flitted between them, before settling on Jimbo. "Where are you from?"

"I told you, he's from my house. He used to live there. In fact, the house is the perfect size. There's only me in the spare bedroom. The master bedroom is free." Clionaisling moved to Jimbo's size and slipped her hand into his. "In fact, we might still have a spare bedroom, if you get my drift."

Jimbo's eyes crinkled as he grinned down at her, showing his perfect, white teeth.

"Your dad's not going to be happy about that at all. You can't just pick up a homeless busker and let him stay with you, no matter how attractive you might find him." Uncle Gerry's face flushed red.

Clionaisling tore her eyes away from Jimbo to her Uncle. "What planet are you living on? He just told you he isn't a busker. You've got him mixed up with someone else."

Why was Uncle Gerry treating her as though she were an immature teenager? Clionaisling fumed. Yes, she was nineteen on the cusp of twenty, but her soul was far more advanced than Uncle Gerry's was, or her father's, or anyone else in the room, with the exception of Jimbo.

"Jimbo and I have only known each other for a short time, but we've been through what most people wouldn't experience in a lifetime," she answered.

"Several lifetimes, in several different planes of existence," Jimbo added.

Uncle Gerry's brow knitted into a single furrow. "Well, I'm going to tell your Da about this, I hope you know. I imagine he'll put his foot right down too."

Time to get right to the point. "Why do you not trust Jimbo? You've been rather cagey around me too, I might add. Care to let me know what's going on?"

Uncle Gerry tugged his moustache with one hand, then ran the same hand through his silver hair. "Alright then. If you're prepared to ask me straight, then I won't beat about the bush. I think your brains are addled because of what happened to your mum. This is a bad time of year for you – and she died, right in this house. In that living room, in fact."

"Oh, so that's what you think is going on?" Clionaisling gritted her teeth. "You think I'm touched in the head and I made this whole thing up, is that right?"

She watched the back of his head nodding. "I do in fact. I heard Jimbo's story in there, all about a journey in an imaginary world, and you know what it sounds like to me? An Alice in Wonderland tall tale made up by a doped up student and her junkie busker boyfriend. You two stink of a strange herb. What have you been smoking, Aisling?"

"For your information, I drank Pixie Pear tea. It's natural – made of hawthorn leaves. You should try some – it's a sedative. Maybe it'll actually help to open your mind for you so you can learn something of the world – before you give yourself a heart attack."

Silence fell. They had both spouted harsh words; Clionaisling knew she shouldn't have allowed herself to get so riled up. She forced her mantra back into her head: *I am safe, I am grounded.*

Uncle Gerry's voice was quieter as he continued. "After your mum died, God rest her soul, your NHS therapy sessions with a psychiatrist stopped when you were thirteen, and your Da didn't want to pay for private sessions, so you had no support to deal with what happened. I don't think you even realise the full extent of what happened. Your guilt and denial have buried the truth so deeply."

Tears sprang to Clionaisling's eyes. "That's where you're wrong. I *do* know what happened, as a matter of fact. Mum didn't have epilepsy. She died because I dropped the plug for the lights in the water bowl under the tree and then unknowingly plugged it in, electrocuting her as she decorated the tree."

Uncle Gerry's face turned as grey as his hair.

"I've been through a lot lately, especially this Christmas. Do you see here?" Clionaisling pointed above her head. "If you were a more enlightened soul yourself, you'd see that my aura has changed colours. I radiate all the colours of the rainbow now as my soul is complete. When I die, I'm going to pass on beyond the sixth plane of existence and reach enlightenment. This is my last earthly journey. But people like you wouldn't know, as you aren't a soul of higher vibration!"

She wiped spit from her bottom lip with the back of her hand. Her voice had risen in anger, but she was above such base emotions; she couldn't let someone without superior knowledge upset her so much. Control. She alone had control of her soul.

"Aisling, that's not all though. What you did to your mum wasn't an accident, you realise? You had been doing a project about electricity at school the week before. You were old enough to know," Uncle Gerry continued.

What was this? An assault on her good character? Uncle Gerry knew nothing. "Are you implying I murdered my mum on purpose?"

He looked alarmed. "I'm not accusing you of that at all. But you have quite a good brain in that head of yours, and you've always had an enquiring mind. Your Da and I think you might have subconsciously been trying to do a science experiment to see what would happen."

Uncle Gerry was wrong. He didn't understand anything.

"It's not the first time you've dabbled with electrocution – you've fried yourself on more than one occasion too."

Electrocution. Yes, she had been zapped by her kettle recently, and deliberately through concocting her brolly-ball-bearings-fairy lights system to aid her journey transcending into the Sidhe Realm; but it had all been for a greater purpose. "Any electrocution I've suffered was for the greater good – I learned from mum's death and applied that knowledge to helping Jimbo. I wouldn't have been able to rescue him from the Sidhe Realm if it weren't for my own personal sacrifice with electricity in order to transport my own soul across into the second plane of existence."

Uncle Gerry's chin wrinkled as his bottom lip turned downwards. He looked defeated. "Jimbo is a homeless man you've picked up in town. I've seen him myself. He's a busker who plays the fiddle, or sometimes a flute. He makes a lot of money because of his good looks and talent – the tourists coming in off the cruise ships must love him. Come on, man," he said to Jimbo, "Tell her the truth, it's not right carrying on like this and you know it."

A frustrated scream rattled out of Clionaisling's throat. She grabbed two bunches of hair with each closed fist on top of her head. "What is your problem?

Why do you need to have an answer for everything? You aren't even listening to me, and now you're insinuating I'm crazy."

A hazy image outside the kitchen window, behind Uncle Gerry's left shoulder, caught Clionaisling's attention. A large, thick oak post with a diameter of at least five feet materialised in a dark, shadowy form. In front of it, two dark wooden thrones that looked like photo-negative versions of reconstructed prehistoric thrones. The side of her brain that held Cliona's memories from the second plane of existence returned to her; she was seeing the interior of the palatial wooden roundhouse at the centre of the crannog in the Sidhe Realm. One throne had belonged to Cliona, and therefore herself. The other throne was for a suitor, a joint ruler. Jimbo.

If she and Jimbo weren't to be appreciated for the higher beings they were, then they would go back to the Sidhe Realm, where a loyal and respectful following awaited them; the fairy folk as they were known on earth. Her loyal Sidhe.

What a shame her wooden roundhouse palace was on the site of Uncle Gerry's house in Finaghy. Of course, she had known this subconsciously all along; in Irish myth and legend, Manannan MacLir and his wife Aoife lived in a palace in modern day Finaghy, now a suburb of Belfast. Manannan had resided there to watch over the Danaan after their defeat by the Milesians, the first Gaels in Ireland. The Danaan had been forced underground into fairy mounds and became known as the Sidhe. Manannan had protected them from mortal eyes by an enchanted mist: the Faeth Fiadha, or Cloak of Concealment and he also controlled the Oilliphéist to restore order, should balance between the Danaan and Milesians ever fail.

Cloak of Concealment. Jimbo had power over the Faeth Fiadha too; it protected him when he needed it.

Clionaisling held up the dowsing rod with holly attached, which she hadn't set down – not once – the whole time she had been in Uncle Gerry's house. Maybe she had kept it for protection – to ward off people who meant her harm. People, not fairies.

"I'm going back to the crannog. Are you coming with me?"

By way of answer, Jimbo held up the other dowsing rod with the hawthorn tethered to it. Clionaisling opened the kitchen door leading into the back garden. As they walked across the grassy lawn of Uncle Gerry's back garden, Jimbo's mysterious mist swirled around them both, cloaking them. Clionaisling reached into the back pocket of her jeans and checked that the fairy lights were still lit in her pocket; they needed the electrical connection to help them transcend from the third plane to the second plane of existence. The last thing she saw before the mist engulfed them both was Uncle Gerry's devastated face through the kitchen window.

Chapter thirty-one

Four months had passed. It was the first of May. Clionaisling touched the fairy lights on her way up the stairwell of her house. It wasn't Christmas, but they would stay up all year round as a beacon to show the way between worlds. They provided some much needed cheer too. Life in the real world was so much more dull and mundane than the Sidhe Realm.

After they had left Uncle Gerry's garden on the second of January, they had stayed in the Sidhe Realm until epiphany: three days. The connection between worlds was at its strongest for twelve days after the solstice; yuletide to the sixth of January. Then they had returned to the physical realm to take care of their responsibilities; as a higher, more evolved being, it was up to Clionaisling to heal the rift with her family.

She understood her uncle's concerns, she just didn't agree with them. Not to mention the fact that he had been a complete ass about it, accusing her of being crazy and having her brains addled by her mum's death. But she would mend their relationship for the sake of the family get-togethers on Boxing Day. She would do it by proof that there were other realms of existence, and not by way of apology.

Dad was likely going to hit the roof about the fact that she had dropped out of her History with Irish course, but the time wasn't right. Seeing Eoin had cemented her decision, enroute to the administration building to start the paperwork for cancellation; the memory of passing Eoin in front of the Queen's University Lanyon Building two weeks previously still gave a fresh sting:

"Hey Eoin. What's the craic?"

Eoin looked behind himself, then back to Clionaisling, confused. "Are you talking to me?"

"I haven't heard from you, it's been a while. Is this about Jimbo?"

Eoin scowled and shrugged his shoulders. "Whatever."

Clionaisling had watched him go. It had to have been his jealousy that she was seeing Jimbo. Eoin had always fancied her, and resented that she had picked Jim Murphy, not him.

But it hurt. It hurt a lot, especially after all they had been through together.

Time to get her head out of the metaphysical for the time being and focus on the real world. Uncle Gerry, dad, Naoise and Jimbo were settled in her living room while she was getting tea and snacks ready. The fact that no conversation filtered through into her kitchen suggested there was an awkward silence that she needed to fix.

Or maybe, dad had beaten her to it. "So, Jim, Aisling tells me business is good? She tells me you're a talented musician?"

Uncle Gerry's eyes flitted to Aisling as she emerged from the kitchen with a tray; his gaze was full of taunting knowledge as though to say, *I was right, your boyfriend is a busker. You both lied to me.*

"It's Clionaisling, dad, I had it legally changed."

Dad closed his eyes, a weary look on his face, but said nothing.

"Yes, I'm bringing in about £100 a day of your modern money," Jimbo said.

"He's more than earning his keep, if that's what you're worried about," Clionaisling quipped.

"No princess, I'm not worried about whether he's paying rent or not, I was just making small talk," said dad.

Clionaisling smiled to herself; an image of one half of herself as dazzling Cliona popped to mind. "Not princess, Queen."

"Queen of the hags," laughed Naoise, pointing at her ketchup-stained jogging trousers.

Clionaisling smiled at her brother. "You're not far wrong. Banshees, not hags."

Or rather, Sidhe, not Banshees. There was nothing terrifying about the fairy folk now that they had been rebalanced by the Oilliphéist, the universe's energy-cleanser.

"Here, Jimbo, you'll have to teach me how to play the fiddle, I could do with £700 a week tax free." Naoise's eyes danced.

Dad clipped his ear. "You're going to focus on your GCSEs and not run the streets, you buck eejit. And please don't be like your sister."

Oh boy. It was coming. Clionaisling dared a glance at her dad.

"You know, it's not too late to restart your course. You don't have to quit. They won't have processed all the paperwork to cancel it yet," said dad, his voice hopeful.

"I've made up my mind. Jimbo and I are going to go travelling with the money he earned from his music."

"Travelling to different planets," Naoise spluttered. He put both index fingers on top of his head, like alien antennas.

"Planes of existence, not planets," she spat. Naoise's smile faltered.

Clionaisling sighed and set down the tray on her coffee table. Such trivial matters, nothing stimulating for the spirit. Time to elevate the conversation to a more enlightened topic. "Mum says hi."

All eyes turned to her, though only Jimbo's were smiling. Not surprising that he was the only one who believed her. "What makes you bring your mum up? You usually only talk about her in the run-up to Christmas?" said dad, a frown on his face.

"Well not anymore. I communicate with her a lot these days. She's still in the Spirit World, but she told me her time is coming soon to return to earth, you know, to be reborn."

"So you really believe all that stuff you said – about the other realms of limbo, or whatnot?" said Uncle Gerry.

"Planes of existence," Clionaisling corrected. "Yes, as a matter of fact, I do. I'm not alone there either, just in case you're still thinking I'm addled. Jimbo believes it and so does Craig. You remember my psychic friend who was in your house back in January?"

Uncle Gerry put his hands up in a gesture of defeat. "Now listen here, love, I didn't come over to your house to get into another fight. I was hoping we could all sit down and iron out a few things – for the sake of the whole family."

"Me too." Clionaisling smiled inwardly; time to show the proof, not apologise. "Let's start by talking about Granda, shall we? Did you know his watch is still working? You know, the one you buried out in your back garden?"

Uncle Gerry blanched. Clionaisling suppressed a chortle; he looked ready to boke his tea and biscuits back up in his own lap. Dad too had turned pale and Naoise looked between all three of them, confusion etched all over his face.

"How did you know about his watch? We buried that millennium time capsule two years before you were born." Uncle Gerry turned to her dad, his face fearful. "Did you ever mention that to her?"

Dad shook his head. "Never. It just never came up."

"Well, the watch started ticking away again just this year, on the sixth of January. It was given a burst of powerful psychokinetic energy."

Twelve days of yuletide, when the energy was strongest.

"That's impossible. It had been broken for a decade when I buried it."

"You buried it in the middle of a lay line. It marks the spot of a huge conjunction of electromagnetic activity." Clionaisling thought of the palatial wooden roundhouse in the Sidhe Realm, where she resided with Jimbo when they returned to the second plane.

Uncle Gerry clearly didn't know what she was talking about, judging by the look on his face. But even that was satisfying enough.

***

Clionaisling's house felt eerie now that everyone had gone; not just dad, Naoise and Uncle Gerry, but Jimbo too. Mayday until the Midsummer solstice; Jimbo had gone back across the realms to appease the ancient spirits that still resided there; the Holly King would prepare to do battle with the Oak King and defeat him, so that after the longest day of the year, the nights would begin to get shorter. Sit under the Maytree on the first of May and you might get taken into the fairy realms. Jimbo had crossed over, body and spirit, through a concoction of Pixie Pear tea and fairy ring mushrooms. Now she was alone, for the time being, until she joined him later that night. But first–

The door knocked. Just on time.

Framed by the inky twilight sky, and a few moths skittering around the outside light, stood Eoin, Liv and Craig on her doorstep.

"Magnificent Clionaisling. Beltaine blessings to thee," said Craig, giving a mock theatrical bow, with a waggle of his hand for added effect.

"Hello glorious leader," said Liv, no less enthusiastically than Craig, though without the pomp and circumstance.

Clionaisling glanced at Eoin last. He offered an awkward smile as he leaned against the doorjamb. "Sorry about a couple of weeks back. That wasn't me. I'm a better friend than that."

"I'm going away for a month. It's a good time to go, now that the midsummer energy is high," said Clionaisling.

Eoin finally spoke. "Is it true that you've quit the course?"

Clionaisling nodded. "I have a greater mission in life than my studies. But it wasn't a waste of time. It got me all youse lot. What would I do without my heterodoxical friends?"

They would follow her to the ends of the earth, and she knew it. Lucky for them, she didn't need them to do so. Believing her, for now, was enough. Three more followers to add to the many thousands of followers she already had waiting for her over in the second realm of existence.

"Are you wanting our help to cross over into the Sidhe Realm once more?" said Craig, holding his chin high at the notion of such a prestigious position to be in.

"No. Not this time. All I need, for once, is a little company," she said.

Liv raised her eyebrows. "You mean, you asked us over just to have – a party?"

Clionaisling shrugged. "Why not? This time last year I didn't have any friends. Now I have the three of you, plus Jimbo, plus an army of Sidhe."

She opened the door wide and let them come inside. As they filed into her living room, Clionaisling glanced up the stairwell, a devious thought popping into her head.

Last Christmas I gave you my heart played this time in her head, not from the speakers at her party, as Clionaisling climbed the stairs to the dark landing. The fairy lights threw a coloured glow over her as she stepped onto the landing.

"Jimbo? Are you there?"

Aisling watched the attic hatch, for old time's sake.

"I'll be joining you later, under the Maytree, before midnight."

In response, the fairy lights on the stairwell flickered. Darkness concentrated on the landing, as a grey-black wavering form began to materialise into a human silhouette. Aisling watched the dark mass of ethereal shadow condense into a figure with broad shoulders that stood around six feet tall.

"Happy Mayday, Jimbo."

Jimbo's dark, shadowy mass closed the distance between them, and Clionaisling felt a tingling sensation touch her lips: a jolt of static electricity. A spirit kiss, since he was now visiting her from the second plane, in ghost form.

"You came just for me, didn't you? You know what a sentimental fool I am," she laughed.

Or maybe kinky. Wasn't it weird to want your boyfriend to materialise in ghost form, just so you could receive a stinging, electrical discharge of a kiss from him?

"Any chance of a little bit more?"

The shadow-ghost before her touched its wavering form against her body, stinging specific parts: just the right parts.

"You know exactly what I like."

Aisling closed her eyes and embraced the sizzle of Jimbo's spirit. Just a taster, until she could have the real thing later.

About the Author:

Leilanie Stewart is an author and poet from Belfast, Northern Ireland. Her writing confronts the nature of self; her novels feature main characters on a dark psychological journey who have a crisis of identity and create a new sense of being. She began writing for publication while working as an English teacher in Japan, a career pathway that has influenced themes in her writing. Her former career as an Archaeologist has also inspired her writing and she has incorporated elements of archaeology and mythology into both her fiction and poetry.

In addition to promoting her own work, Leilanie runs Bindweed Magazine, a creative writing literary journal with her writer husband, Joseph Robert. Aside from publishing pursuits, Leilanie enjoys spending time with her husband and their lively literary lad, a voracious reader of books featuring creatures of the deep.

Acknowledgements

Thank you to my hubby and editor, Joseph Robert, for all the detailed feedback on this story, from when The Fairy Lights first started life as a short story back in December 2021 all the way through to the finished novel. You always give my books the shine they need.

Thanks also to little KJ for being my publishing assistant and clicking the forward button, allowing me to check formatting on each page of the finished manuscript. What an amazing editorial helper you are. I always love to hear that "Author Mummy writes books for grown-ups" too.

I'm grateful to all the following people: Heather for the fantastic proofreading work as always; Amy Jeffrey and Ellen Collier for being fabulous beta readers; Shona Armstrong, Suchitra Varma, Kendra Sneddon, Jeanne Bertille, Sarah Stockman and Zeena for all the support.

Last, but not least, thanks to you, for buying my book. Having readers keeps me motivated to write more stories, so just to let you know that I appreciate you taking the time to read and review my books. It means more than you know.

Other books by Leilanie Stewart

The Blue Man

Two best friends. An urban legend. A sinister curse.

Twenty years ago, horror loving Sabrina told her best friend, Megan, the terrifying Irish folk tale of the Blue Man, who sold his soul to the Devil in vengeance against a personal injustice. What should have been the best summer of their schooldays turned into a waking nightmare, as the Blue Man came to haunt Megan. Sabrina, helpless to save Megan from a path of self-destruction and substance abuse as she sought refuge from the terror, left Belfast for a new life in Liverpool.

Twenty years later, the former friends reunited thinking they had escaped the horrors of the past. Both were pregnant for the first time. Both had lived elsewhere and moved back to their hometown, Belfast. Both were wrong about the sinister reality of the Blue Man, as the trauma of their school days caught up to them – and their families.

Why did the Blue Man terrorise Megan? Was there more to the man behind the urban legend? Was their friendship – and mental health – strong enough to overcome a twenty year curse?

The Buddha's Bone

Death

Kimberly Thatcher wasn't an English teacher. She wasn't a poet. She wasn't an adventurer. Now she wasn't even a fiancée. But when one of her fellow non-Japanese colleagues tried to make her a victim, she said no.

Cremation

In Japan on a one-year teaching contract at a private English language school, and with her troubled relationship far behind her in London, Kimberly set out to make new friends. She would soon discover the darker side of travelling alone – and people's true intentions.

Rebirth

As she came to question the nature of all those around her – and herself – Kimberly was forced to embark on a soul-searching journey into emptiness. What came next after you looked into the abyss? Could Kimberly overcome the trauma – of sexual assault and pregnancy loss – blocking her path to personal enlightenment along the way, and forge a new identity in a journey of-

Death. Cremation. Rebirth.

Gods of Avalon Road

London, present day.

Kerry Teare and her university friend Gavin move to London to work for the enigmatic Oliver Doncaster. Their devious new employer lures them into an arcane occult ritual involving a Golden Horse idol.

Britannia, AD 47.

Aithne is the Barbarian Queen of the Tameses tribes. The Golden Warrior King she loves is known as Belenus. But are the mutterings of the Druids true: is he really the Celtic Sun God himself?

Worlds collide as Oliver's pagan ritual on Mayday summons gods from the Celtic Otherworld of Avalon. Kerry is forced to confront the supernatural deities and corrupt mortals trying to control her life and threatening her very existence.

Printed in Great Britain
by Amazon